The Last Word
&
Other Stories

A Sheila-Na-Gig Anthology

Edited by John Bullock

Contents

The Last Word

In my shop, The Last Word, the romance novels live on shelves next door to the children's books. They seem to like each other, believing as they both do in the possibility of happiness. Their proximity has caused some alarm and confusion, though—patrons want to know why these half-naked men with their oily chests are shoulder to shoulder with picture books about bear families and talking pickles. It's true that some of the children who come in for Saturday afternoon story hour stare in wonder at these men and their tousle-haired paramours in petticoats and tight bodices. "No harm in looking," I say to my critics. "It's the books about warfare you should worry about, the violence and bloodbaths in them, the bad food and body lice."

Over time, I've been labeled an eccentric by a few of the mirthless souls who come into the store, some of whom have spent entire afternoons clogging up an aisle while they read a book from cover to cover, apparently mistaking The Last Word for the library. When criticized for the layout of my store, I point out that I sell books about confused moose who think they're kittens, about doughnuts that speak Chinese and know how to knit. How dangerous can I possibly be?

I have two full-time employees, Henry and Judy, and between the three of us, we keep the store skipping along. When Henry's son Ben is home from college for summer breaks and for the December holidays, which is the time of year we're currently cresting, he puts in 15 or 20 hours too. I need a body on the sales floor and another for gift-wrapping and checkout. They're each good with the cash register, more patient and gently parental, than I am—it is an old machine and turns to stone if you key in the numbers too quickly. Judy has nicknamed it Attila, which might be part of the problem. It's been said machines have souls. My guess is that Attila's is in purgatory, considering how thin-skinned and vindictive he can be. Admittedly, there are many mysteries in the world. What happens next? What happens when we're dead? When we run out of money? Whatever question a person might ask, I can guarantee there's a book out there trying to answer it.

It's Ben, Henry's offspring, who had a big idea I decided earlier this month to test out because I like him and his enviably renewable energy. "Bookseller recommendations," he said, smiling winningly, knowing I can be reluctant to try new things because, inevitably, they mean new work. Still, I decided it was long overdue—I've known for a while that other stores do it, but by temperament, I am not an eager joiner. In any case, I gave in, and voilà, shelf cards, paper-thin squares of wisdom and wit meant to seduce indecisive or desultory shoppers into leaping upon a title and making it their own. I wrote the first slew of them, taped them to the shelves under each book. These are a few of the highlights:

> *The Death of Ivan Ilych*: What's not to love?
> *The Gulag Archipelago*: Something for everyone, friends!
> *The Joy of Cooking*: Not for the faint of heart.

"Interesting take," says Ben, bemused but smiling, when he spots the Gulag card, Solzhenitsyn's forced labor of love. It's a little before nine in the morning, ten days before Christmas, a Friday. We're preparing to open, and I can already see a few people outside waiting for me to throw open the door.

"What I wrote is true, isn't it?" I say. "This book is about the triumph of the human spirit over tyranny. As the card says, 'Something for everyone.'" I pull a copy of *Gulag* off the shelf and hold it up between us.

"That's really what you think?" he asks, polite as always. "I haven't read much of it, but I thought it was more about the monotony of evil. I hope this doesn't sound presumptuous, but maybe you should put on the card what you just said instead of what's on there now."

"That makes the book sound like self-help."

"I don't know, but you could—"

"I need to think about this some more. Maybe it's not the best candidate for an inaugural staff pick." I put this chunk of a book back and remove the shelf tag before I go up to the front where Judy stands behind Attila, cracking open a roll of quarters, Ben on my heels.

"I'm sorry if I'm overstepping, Cathy," he says.

I turn and look at up him. He's at least five inches taller than I am, skinny as Jack Sprat but he's got the kind of face—dark eyes, long lashes, a head full of golden brown curls—that keeps the hopeful, bookish girls coming back to shyly gape at him, wondering if he's their Mr. Darcy. "Not at all. It's good you're thinking about this. If everyone thought the same way, I'd be out of business. Look at all these conflicts, controversies, and fantasies," I say. "All of it beginning in the agitated minds of our major and minor writers." I gesture toward the tables closest to Attila, the new hardcovers in fiction and nonfiction—this is the store's money shot, such as it is. No idiosyncratic placements like the children's books and romance novels (or the cookbooks, which sell at a brisk clip regardless of where I place them—right now they live next to a display of titles about natural disasters—I've never been good at cooking).

Judy, a retired surgical nurse who is presently rereading Penelope Fitzgerald's novels *The Blue Flower* and *The Bookshop* for what must be the third time since she started working for me, glances up from the register. She's counting singles now that the coins have been liberated from their rolls. "Robby Cotter is out there," she says. "Are you letting him in?"

Robby has been caught twice for attempting to steal the same book, *Be My Flower: A Poetry Collection for Romantic Souls*. It is not an expensive book, and the second time I caught him, I almost let him take it home, but if I'd done this, word would probably have gotten around I was a soft touch. I have not read this poetry collection and therefore cannot comment on its merits, but Robby was almost in tears both times he was stopped on his way out the door, apologizing repeatedly and begging for amnesty. He's in his thirties and designs websites, but not enough of them, from what I can tell, or else he charges too little. He has an older brother in Indiana who manages a wolf refuge, a story I questioned until Judy confirmed it online. All this is information he's shared during his many visits to the store, pre-*Be My Flower* theft attempts, the second occurring a little over two weeks ago.

I look over at the entrance, and there indeed is Robby standing a few feet behind three other people waiting to be let in. His lumpy navy blue parka is unzipped, the T-shirt he's wearing visible. I've seen him in this shirt before—it shows a surly cat holding a cell phone, the caption: "If cats could text you back, they wouldn't."

"Didn't you ban him from the store until after the holidays?" asks Judy, peering at me over the top of her glasses.

"I made the mistake of telling him he could come back if he wore a catsuit."

From the look on Ben's face, it's clear he isn't sure how to interpret this.

Judy chuckles. "One thing I'll say about working here, I'm never bored."

I catch Ben's eye. "Aren't catsuits skin-tight? Nowhere to hide stolen property. He must think his cat T-shirt's a good substitute."

"You want me to go talk to him?" he asks.

"No, I'll do it," I say. This is my proverbial mess, since I didn't call the police when I caught him stealing *Be My Flower*. Twice. It's only his conscience and whatever respect he has for authority, i.e. me, keeping him out of here.

I unlock the door. It isn't nine yet, but we're only two minutes shy of the hour. Although small business ownership essentially requires it, I try not to be a nitpicker.

"Good morning, everyone." I smile and catch the eye of each of the three customers who aren't Robby. "We're all in this together," I say, eliciting a little laughter.

Robby hasn't moved from where he was skulking behind the other early patrons. "I brought you this," he says, holding out a red envelope. "To say I'm sorry."

"It's not necessary," I say, noticing he's spelled my name with a K instead of a C. "But thank you."

He nods, his face as crimson as the envelope.

"I can't let you in the store, Robby. You're not wearing a catsuit, and it's not the new year yet. But I do like your T-shirt."

"I have money," he says, unearthing a twenty from his parka's front pocket. "Can I buy something from out here?"

"What would you like?" I wonder if he's finally ready to pay for *Be My Flower*, but we sold the one copy we had in stock last week to a teenage girl who informed me as I wrestled with Attila that the author was soon releasing a sequel, *Be My Cloud*.

"One of those little notebooks. The expensive kind. Their covers are mole skin, right?"

"Moleskine," I say. "They're not actually made from moles."

"I'd like a red one, if you have them in that color. Whatever size a twenty will cover." He gives me a half abashed, half proud look. "I've started writing poetry. Your store should have a poetry group. I could lead it. I wouldn't charge you. How about on Sunday afternoons?"

"That's one of the busiest days here, so not Sundays," I say. "I'll think about it, Robby. No guarantees."

"I could do it on a weeknight," he says.

"We'll see."

"My brother has a new wolf. Her name is Ella," he announces when I return with his notebook and change a few minutes later. "He thinks I should come live with him, but I don't want to."

"You're your own man," I say.

"I am." His face glows with conviction. "I definitely am."

For a second it looks like he's going to hug me, and I take an involuntary step back. He sees this and whatever impulse is there is snuffed out. I'm not a hugger, unlike my ex-husband, who will hug anyone, anywhere. The last time I remember him hugging me, however, was two and a half years ago when I told him he could take our four All-Clad pans with him when he moved out. I felt terribly guilty about divorcing him, my first and only divorce, his second and counting, since he's now engaged to be married a third time. Somehow, we've managed to stay friendly. He comes into the store every month or so and buys new hardcovers. I could have done worse than staying married to him, I suppose, but he did not know how to save a dime; a favorite hobby of his was opening new credit card accounts. There was also the fact the house would have become a pigpen if I hadn't been run interference, along with running the dishwasher and the vacuum in between running a bookstore. Steve and I are much better off as friends, although I'm still paying off two of his erstwhile credit cards.

As I'm about to step back into the store, Robby says, "If I came back wearing a catsuit would you really let me inside?"

"Yes, but if you get sticky fingers again, this time I will call the police. And you'll need to give me your coat while you're in the store."

"You're pretty, Cathy," he says.

This takes me aback. It's not that I think I'm homely, but I no longer spend much time primping in the morning, not like I did well into college when I paid a lot more attention to bongs and booze than to books. This began to change when a close friend fell into the Potomac and drowned while riding his bicycle home from a very drunken party.

"Thank you, Robby," I say.

"You are," he says. "Were you homecoming queen in high school?"

I can't help but laugh. "I was not."

"You should have been!"

"I have to get back to it," I say, leaving him where he stands clutching his bright new Moleskine, its cellophane as yet unbreached.

"I promise I won't try to steal anything ever again," I hear him say as the door closes behind me.

From her post behind Attila, Judy gives me a wry look. "I couldn't help but overhear. Do you think he has a crush on you?"

"I very much doubt it." I lower my voice when I notice one of the other early customers, a man with a hickory cane I've seen in here before, eyeing us from the gardening section a few yards away. "He's just an odd duck," I whisper to Judy.

"He can still have a crush on you."

"Trying to steal from me is not the best way to win my heart."

"Do They Know It's Christmas?" plays innocuously through the dusty speakers that Steve, in a spasm of uxoriousness, suspended from three of the store's corners a few years ago, probably hoping to forestall our separation. Several more customers have arrived since we've opened, and over at the table piled high with boxed holiday cards, there's a companionable murmur between two women dressed for yoga or Zumba or pole-dancing or whatever it is the fitness moguls are currently making millions hawking.

"Did you know this song is almost forty years old?" says the man in the gardening section, pointing up at one of the speakers.

Judy and I look over at him. If he's right, I was all of five or six when it came out. My mother bought the 45 and played it innumerable times the first couple of Christmases after its release, nearly driving my father round the bend.

"Forty years. Goodness," Judy exclaims.

"Reagan was in the White House," says the man, venomous. "What a shit show that was. Bet the old fool didn't read one book after he was out of high school." He shakes his head and turns away. Judy catches my eye, laughing a little. "He's probably right about Reagan and his reading habits."

"If only it were funny," I say.

We both laugh.

The man scoffs. "He never should have been elected! Read Roger Perlstein's *Reaganland* if you haven't yet."

"Rick Perlstein," says Judy.

"Roger," he says.

"It's Rick," she insists. She's right. I haven't read it, but it's on my towering to-be-read pile.

The man grumbles something neither of us can decipher. She gives me a coy smile as she tells me she can handle the front for now, freeing me to go into the back where, in my tiny office, I open Robby's card. On the front is a picture of a cartoon dog trying to cozy up to a very spiny, frowning cactus. Inside it reads: Oops! I knew I shouldn't have done that. Robby has also included a note:

Dear Kathy,

Your store is one of my top three favorite places in the world. I shouldn't have tried to steal *Be My Flower* (twice), but I was pretty broke for a while. When I was a kid I stole some 5-cent pieces of bubble gum from the gas station, but other than that, I haven't stolen anything else in my entire life. I hope you can forgive me. I will do whatever it takes to make it up to you.

Love, Robby

PS: My other two favorite places in the world are Wrigley Field and the chocolate factory by my grandma's house in Frankfort, Indiana.

I put the card in my desk. I don't really know what to think, except for what I'm certain is true: everyone suffers. When I see Robby next, which for all I know could be later today, he'll say whatever he's going to say, and in reply I'll say whatever strikes me as appropriate. This, more or less, sums up the verbal commerce of our lives. Sometimes we say the least appropriate thing and make an enemy for life. Other times we say precisely the right thing and the world is burnished, our bodies limber and invincible for a little while.

After my friend drowned and I stopped going out every night like it was my vocation, I thought I'd become a writer, but after a few years I realized I wasn't very good at ignoring all the rejection and self-doubt. I became a librarian and did that job for twelve years, until I inherited some money a decade ago from my own grandmother who did not live near a chocolate factory (the one in her Wisconsin town made washers and dryers). I bought a bookstore when the owners put it up for sale and retired to Sun City, Arizona. I changed the name from Book Bonanza to The Last Word, and here I still am.

There are days when I want to sell to the highest bidder and move to a place where it's warm all year too, where no one will return a book it's obvious from the shape it's in they've read every word of. No one will complain my prices are too high, or ask why the hell it takes a week to get a book. They can just order it online and it'll be on their doorstep tomorrow! To these people, I wish I could say what I'm really thinking, which is some variety of You really have no clue, asshole.

I don't see myself leaving, however. For one, with so many books at arm's length, I'm rarely lonely. It took me a while to realize this, but when I did, I understood a lot about myself, and about other people who love books too. I also understood a few things about the people who don't. If only I could show them how much they're missing. But of course a woman has to pick her battles.

The day passes in a flurry of minor tasks and one or two major nuisances. Attila locks up as I'm entering the purchases of a customer buying $280 worth of children's books, romance novels, and holiday cards, but Judy is able to coax our resident mechanical sociopath back into submission. With Ben's help, I inventory the past week's deliveries and sort through dozens of the galleys publishers have sent us in the last couple of months, saving some, putting others in bags for the Salvation Army. (There is never, ever enough space. If *Hoarders* needs new blood, the small bookstore is a good candidate.)

The highlight of the afternoon: I do a quick tally and discover we're more than three thousand dollars ahead of last year in sales. Thank you, Prince Harry. This puts me in the best mood I've been in for weeks, and I write a few new shelf cards and hand them off to Ben who passes no visible judgement.

The Bridges of Madison County: One of the few instances of a movie surpassing the book it's based on (in fairness to the author, if it weren't for his book, the movie wouldn't exist).

American Heritage Dictionary: A real page-turner!

Zen and the Art of Motorcycle Maintenance: See what all the fuss is about (and then please enlighten me).

It's ten minutes after eight, just past closing, when Robby returns. Henry, who came in when Ben clocked out at two, alerts me to his arrival. He's behind Attila, counting the drawer.

I see that Robby isn't wearing a catsuit beneath his old parka for this visit either, but he's holding a copy of *Be My Flower* in one hand, his new red notebook in the other. I'm tired and want to go home but I open the door.

"Can I read you a poem I wrote?" he asks.

Oh God, I think, suppressing a sigh. "I see you have a copy of *Be My Flower*," I say.

"I ordered it online," he says, sheepish. "But I got it through Bookshop.org, not the other place that shall not be named. It came this afternoon."

"You can read me your poem, but first, come inside." It's a cold night, snow in the air.

"Are you sure?" He looks so hopeful, my better nature insists I go along.

I glance over at Henry, who's trying to keep a straight face. "Come in," I say. "But just for a minute. We're closing up for the night."

Robby is freshly shaven, his body jittery with the suspense and pleasure of having found someone to hear his new poem. "You and Henry ready?" he asks.

"We are," I say.

"First, I want to give you this." He hands me *Be My Flower*. "For the store. I bought two copies." He opens his notebook. "Okay. Here goes."

He clears his throat and in a clear, measured voice—he must have practiced—he reads his poem.

Bookstore

You are like a lamp
lighting our town, lighting
every window of every house,
each book on your shelves
a little lantern, each sentence,
each line, a magic spell.
You are like spring after a long winter,
like a flowering tree always blooming
in the middle of our lives.

It's a very corny poem, but I have tears in my eyes when he stops. "That's beautiful," I manage to say, just barely. "Thank you for reading it to us."

"Nice job, Robby," says Henry. "I think we've got our poet laureate of The Last Word."

The look on Robby's face is incandescent. He presses the notebook to his chest and says, voice quavering, "This is now my favorite place in the world. After the chocolate factory and Wrigley Field."

Before I realize what I'm doing, my arms are around him, *Be My Flower* and the Moleskine pressed between us, the spicy scent of his shaving lotion commingling with the must of his old parka and the night's cold humidity. "Keep writing," I say softly. "Just don't try to steal any more books."

"I won't," he says, emphatic.

"We'll see about the poetry group," I say, pulling back. "I'll let you know."

Driving home, I wonder how many good days we can expect, and if some of us, by sheer force of will, can simply pull them out of the ether. I've never thought of myself as an optimist, but I suppose that owning a bookstore means I am one. Every day I get to unlock the doors and turn on the lights and ask myself, Who will come into the store today? Which music will I play? What do I want to read next?

Setter Brindle Birch

Facing Superhawk

Spring 2012.

That's Louise, marching down the center aisle into the auditorium, where a well-dressed businesswoman is about to speak.

Louise must be in her sixties now, and her hair is short and spiky. Mint green, and the roots don't show anymore. I know that's her because I've seen her face so many times these past three years—in the papers, on TV, and on social media. She's nothing like the Louise I remember.

We met years ago at a training workshop, when I was still a student intern at the old location. The Louise I met that day was dumpy, lumpy, and graceless. Now she's almost . . . elegant. She's almost regal.

***

Winter 1997.

Quigley leads the two-day workshop at a community center near the office, and I'm one of maybe a dozen participants from around the province. Like them, I'm eager to learn about the animal welfare legislation and how it's enforced.

With twenty years behind him, Quigley knows better than anyone what kindness emissaries can and can't do. A breeder can keep dogs in cages twenty-four hours a day as long as the cages are clean. A farmer can shoot a neighbor's dog for "worrying livestock." Blowing marijuana smoke up a dog's nose might result in a drug conviction, but a cruelty charge probably won't stick. Someone would have to prove the dog didn't like it.

"We're all animal people," Quigley says. "We want to see animal abusers hung by their toes. That's not going to happen."

I listen in silence, taking it all in. So does everyone. The only person to raise any objections is a woman in the third row wearing purple sunglasses. She's slightly overweight, with crazy disheveled hair under a biker's cap, and she's brought an enormous shopping cart with her to the workshop.

"Pathetic!" The woman shouts it at no one in particular.

"Excuse me?" says Quigley. "Was there a question?"

"You heard me!" she answers. "PAAA-THET-IC! Prove the dog didn't like it? Give me a break."

Quigley is used to this kind of thing. You can tell. Outbursts like this are part of the job, nothing he hasn't seen before.

"Of all the charges we file, eighty-seven percent result in convictions," he says. "That's a lot better than the police."

"That's 'cause you take on the easy cases!" the woman shoots back. "It stinks!"

Quigley goes on as if she weren't there. "There's a reason for that. We don't waste time and money on cases that don't stand a chance."

He moves on to dogfighting. Without exception, all dogs seized in dogfighting investigations have to be killed. Explaining the policy, Quigley cites the highest authority in the field: the renowned behavioral scientist Roy Austin. Dr. Austin, who works at one of the big US charities, is prepared to testify against any organization that adopts out a fighting dog and subsequently becomes the target of a lawsuit.

In all his years with the Kindness Kickstart, Quigley tells the group, he's never seen a fighting dog who was aggressive toward people. "The problem is aggression toward other animals."

Tentatively, I raise my hand. "What if the dog goes to a very responsible home, without any other animals? What if the family guarantees the dog will never leave the property? That he'll never come into contact with other animals?"

Quigley looks stung. Have I said something wrong?

"I don't think that's much of a life for a dog."

Still, I press him. "But the dog would have human companionship. He could play ball with the family in a fenced backyard. Um, right?"

Quigley shakes his head. "We ran scenarios like that past Dr. Austin. He said he'd testify against us."

During the break, I approach the woman in sunglasses. She's at the refreshment table, peering closely at the label on a box of cookies.

"Do you work at one of the branches?" I ask her.

The woman just laughs. "You must have read about me in the papers," she says after a moment. "Or maybe you were too young. My name is Louise Hawke. I used to be the CEO."

***

Spring 2012.

I remember seeing Louise's name in the newspapers when I was still in high school, but I never paid much attention in those days. What stayed with me, somewhere in the back of my mind, was a short profile in a glossy women's magazine that I found by chance in the school library.

Louise wanted a world without liver pâté, according to the magazine. Without hamburgers or lamb chops or meatloaf. Without ice cream or custard or cake (because the eggs and milk in the cake came from animals), and without circuses or zoos or ivory piano keys. No fur coats or footballs, and no more animal-tested pills with bovine coatings.

Not even bovine coatings.

I can't remember if I was already avoiding meat by the time I saw that article—if so, it was just the visible chunks. The big changes came later, or at least they seemed like big changes at the time.

The tone of the article was somewhat flippant, as I recall. Or was that a misreading on my part? Had the journalist meant to poke fun at Louise or to pay her a sort of quirky tribute? Maybe an editor injected the snark.

***

Winter 1997.

On the second day of the workshop, Louise's presence is noxious. All morning, she looks for chances to upstage Quigley. She practices dance moves and assumes yoga postures as he's talking. She prances around like a cheerleader, saying, "Rah-rah-rah!" She does arabesques and demi-pliés in front of the projector, partly blocking the screen. She even sneaks up behind him and puts her index fingers behind his head, childishly pretending to give him devil horns.

The biker's cap is gone and now everyone at the workshop can see that Louise's thick, chin-length hair is graying at the roots. She's dyed it two gaudy, mismatched shades of canary yellow and botched the job. She must have used nail scissors to cut her bangs since the last session, and the results aren't flattering. She wears faded army surplus pants and a flannel shirt with splotches on it. I wonder what the splotches are, but I make myself look away.

"You got dressed up today," says Quigley as the afternoon session starts. Is he talking to me or Louise? Uncertain, I smile nervously and smooth out my thrift store skirt, hoping the wrinkles don't show. Louise doesn't acknowledge Quigley, but only leans forward and touches her toes.

Quigley still has a lot of material to cover. He begins by summarizing the legal changes the Kindness Kickstart is working toward, and then he explains why the political process has been stalled for the past decade.

"I could never be a politician," he says wearily. "We worked with one of the MPs, Miranda Elmer, for about five years. She introduced a bill to update the Criminal Code just so it would spell out in twentieth-century language the things that everyone, everywhere, already finds reprehensible. Starving a dog to death. Setting a cat on fire. Dumping puppies by the side of the road.

"Every time Miranda raised the issue in parliament, backbenchers shouted her down. They thought she was proposing some animal rights bill that was going to outlaw farming, when nothing could have been further from the truth."

Louise puts her hands over her mouth as if suppressing an urge to vomit, then lurches forward and clutches her chest. I ignore her and listen to Quigley.

"The bill died on the table when the deadline passed," Quigley continues, and Louise begins shaking. For the first time, she takes off her sunglasses. Her gray eyes are glassy, and she's staggering as if she's drunk or high.

"Animal rightists did more harm than good when the bill was being debated," Quigley goes on, apparently unconcerned that Louise is curled up in the fetal position, hyperventilating on the floor.

"The bill wouldn't have made anything illegal that wasn't already illegal," he says as Louise's arms flail around. After a moment she throws her head back, and then her whole body goes limp.

"But the damn protest signs scared the MPs," he says. "They wouldn't touch our bill as long as the bunny huggers were supporting it too."

Louise is lying there unresponsive. I look at Quigley, then back at the room. Everyone is leafing through their notes.

Should I get up and check her breathing? Ask Quigley to call an ambulance?

"So now we're back to the drawing board."

As soon as Quigley says it, Louise sits bolt upright and shakes the room with a burst of demoniacal cackling. I want to say something now because she's really distracting me, and I'm having trouble focusing on the lecture, but no one else seems to notice she's there. Like all the other trainees, I do my best to shut out this eccentric woman and her—I don't know what to call it. Performance art?

Before giving the exam, Quigley wraps up the lesson. "I used to ask myself why the Kindness Kickstart had the words 'prevent cruelty' in its mission statement. I'd say to myself, We don't prevent anything. We wait until it's already happened."

Using a chair as a stepladder, Louise climbs onto my desk. Hands in the air, face animated, she makes a solemn announcement.

"Ladies and gentlemen," she tells an invisible audience way off in the distance behind Quigley's head. "You may rest assured of one thing in this world. We don't prevent anything!"

She's mimicking his way of talking. The senior kindness emissary has an affable, jovial manner, but his words sound ugly and rough coming from this ragamuffin heckler. He's trying to ignore her, but I know she's making him uncomfortable.

"We wait until it's already happened!" Louise sings the line in a high, mocking voice that echoes off the walls and leaves a queasy feeling in the pit of my stomach.

Quigley's trying to speak, but Louise won't let him. She waves her arms, fists clenched, and repeats his words in a snarl while stomping her feet. She reminds me of that little girl in *The Exorcist* so many years ago. Then, deadpan, she says, "We should change our mission statement because it's a goddamned lie."

With that she lets her head drop forward, as if waiting for unseen stage lights to fade, and shrivels up like a tired old plant before sinking back into her seat.

Everyone's eyes remain glued to Quigley at the podium. No one acknowledges Louise, and I'm no exception. Determined to pass the exam, I pretend not to see her there at the periphery of my vision. Quigley picks up where he left off and concludes the lecture without missing a beat.

"But then I thought about it," he says. "And I realized that the founders of the Kindness Kickstart, a hundred and twenty-odd years ago, were ahead of their time. We can't prevent all cruelty to animals, but we can prevent many animals from suffering more and worse cruelty. And that's all we can do."

Louise just slumps in her seat and makes loud farting noises with her mouth. Then I see the police uniform out of the corner of my eye, and suddenly Louise's defiance is gone. Now she's pleading with the officer as they talk quietly by the window. While Quigley hands out exam papers, Louise takes her shopping cart and the burly policeman follows her out. I want to look, but I keep my eyes on my paper.

***

Spring 2012.

Before social media, Louise was just another burnt-out activist. People called her nutty, radical, unkempt. There were rumors that she'd broken into a lab in the seventies. When I first started as a student intern, a few people mentioned her in passing. To the old-timers around here she was an embarrassing relic from the early days, a reminder of the Kindness Kickstart's awkward adolescence.

For a long time she obliged everyone by fading into obscurity, but now she's back in the public eye as the leader of Bastet. What started as a cat rescue group in the seventies has evolved into a disruptive, in-your-face vegan performance art troupe. Three years ago, an art student won a prize for designing Bastet's ubiquitous turquoise and gold logo, a sleek line drawing of a cat with an Egyptian collar and a nose ring. It's plastered all over the city now, in the subways and on walls every few blocks in the art district and near the university.

Today Louise has nothing on but a bottle-green leotard and footless tights under an oversize Bastet T-shirt. She's lost weight, I see when I get a closer look. She looks like she could take any of us in a fight.

***

Winter 1997.

I pass the exam with a score of ninety percent, including bonus points for knowing a vizsla is a dog and an Abyssinian is a cat. I get my kindness emissary card, and a few weeks later I run into Louise again. Some cat rescuers are having a potluck at a community center downtown, and I've come to see what it's all about. It's a weekend and I'm here on my own, not for work.

To my surprise, Louise is the organizer. She still has her shopping cart, but when I look closely I see that it isn't a shopping cart at all—it's an oversize animal carrier with a bony calico cat inside. Bastet, named after the Egyptian goddess, has a plastic tube coming out of one nostril and a plastic cone on her head. The carrier is just big enough for Bastet and the medical supplies she needs to stay alive.

"She needs special care," Louise says when she sees me looking. "Meds four times a day, eye drops, an inhaler, sub-Q fluids, constant supervision. She must be at least twenty-four by now."

The presentation is a history lesson. The rescue group, named after the cat in the carrier, started during a labor strike in the seventies. Louise was one of eight shelter volunteers who crossed the picket lines to keep the animals alive.

"We were called all kinds of vile names," she tells the group. "We even had dead animals thrown at us." All this happened across the parking lot from the office where I work, and I'm shocked that I've never heard about it before.

"Which is understandable," Louise continues, "but there were precious lives at stake."

After that, we all learn, Louise and a few colleagues conspired to take over the troubled organization where they'd started out as lowly volunteers. By the mid-eighties they'd built up a power base. Finally, they could implement bold shelter reform plans and push through a province-wide no-kill policy.

With Louise in an upper management role, the Kindness Kickstart established affordable spay-neuter clinics in five cities and made plans to expand the service to eight more within the next three years. When the veterinarians' association sued, alleging unfair business practices, Louise and her colleagues fought back and won.

"They accused us of taking business away from private vet clinics," Louise explains. "Which of course was utter bullshit, because our clinics served poor communities that couldn't afford to take their animals to private vets. Dogs and cats were allowed to breed free in those communities, and illnesses and injuries were going untreated.

"The Supreme Court agreed with us. They told the vets to go fuck themselves." The crowd laughs and cheers.

"You're paraphrasing the judge, right, Louise?" someone asks. More laughs.

Upon taking over as CEO, Louise immediately went to work on the antiquated policy statements. Her new forward-looking policy direction emphasized vegan education, affordable vet care, opposition to animals in entertainment, and opposition to vivisection.

"Well," she says, "we lasted six months."

When Louise presented her revised policy statements to the board of directors for approval, she tells the group, the board scheduled an emergency meeting to debate what it saw as a radical change of direction.

"The venue was packed," she recalls. "Reporters were there. Industry pressure groups were watching the proceedings intently."

Under more scrutiny than ever before in the organization's hundred-year history, the board caved. In one day, three board members stepped down, Louise's policy statements were scrapped, and the chairman led an entire team of reform-minded executives out of the building.

After that came a decade of conservative leadership. There would be no more challenges to institutionalized animal abuse, no more subsidized veterinary services, and no changes to the policy statements. The existing statements dated back to the 1920s—the language was so flowery and convoluted that board members spent entire meetings debating the nuances of a line or a subparagraph. With its counter-coup, the new leadership had blessed the status quo and set it in cement.

I put twenty dollars in Bastet's donation box and head for the bus stop.

***

Summer 2012.

Louise has had many successors, each one with a new vision and a new plan to improve things.

"This is a wise-use organization," Pim declared upon taking the helm two years ago. Now, relaunching the magazine after a long hiatus, he repeats himself. No animal rights terms like "vegan" or "speciesism" or "cruelty-free" are to appear on our pages ever again—not even the back page. There will be no further contact with any freelance writers associated with "the animal rights fringe."

"Your job is to clean up the grammar and spelling," Pim says. "That's it."

Pim and Quigley think alike where the magazine is concerned, and there's no use fighting. I'm lucky I'm allowed to help with the editorial side at all—twice a week, as long as it doesn't interfere with my responsibilities in the mailroom. It's that or quit, and I don't have another job to go to.

***

Spring 2012.

The magazine still reflects a conservative mindset. In a big feature earlier this year, over my objections, we praised portable slaughterhouses. The lead article for the upcoming issue applauds the "pork partnership," an agreement to cooperate with pig farmers on a new labeling system. I protested meekly but got nowhere. That's why I came to the university with Quigley this morning, to take notes.

Spring 2012.

Louise is with a dozen or so activists in matching T-shirts. Together, they invade the auditorium in a V formation. Each one is holding some kind of package or bundle, but I can't make out the shapes from here.

Louise has a bullhorn in one hand and a bundle in her other arm. It's pressed up close to her chest.

The woman at the podium is stunned; she glances nervously at the emcee.

Before the activists barged in, this woman was about to introduce a seven-point strategy to make the pork industry more humane. After a moment's hesitation, she breaks the silence.

"The thought of sending pigs to slaughter," she begins, "speaking as a farmer who raises pigs from the time they're this big, is not something I like to think about."

It's jarring to hear that from someone in the business of killing animals to sell their flesh. It's a little unnerving, too, that this slaughter apologist is so soft-spoken and relatable. If I'd met her somewhere else, I'd probably like her.

Her voice falters. The activists are advancing down the aisle.

"The use of animals for food may be totally unacceptable to some of you," the speaker continues. "Maybe you don't eat meat. Maybe you don't use animal products at all and have chosen other lifestyles. But I want to say—as a farmer—that we care about the animals we raise. We love them, even, in a way. Only—they're not pets."

Rattled, she stops speaking. The emcee marches down the steps and stares the activists down. "Is there a problem?"

No response. The protesters walk past him, up the steps and onto the stage. The well-dressed pork industry representative, wide-eyed and incredulous, steps aside.

The activists have rehearsed well, and their movements are synchronized. It isn't until they take over the stage that I see what they're holding: animals. A chicken. A lamb. A duck. An octopus. A tiny yellow chick, completely still and curled up in a woman's hand.

For a moment, the audience is mute. Then a few people stand up; some are whispering and others are yelling. Some are in the aisles and others just sit and watch, not knowing what else to do. I sit and watch.

"This is Dora," Louise says into the microphone, ignoring the commotion. She's cradling a lifeless chicken in her arms.

"What is this?" the emcee yells. "You can't disrupt our—"

"Dora was found during a night visit to a free-range farm," Louise says before the organizers cut power to the microphone. She switches to the bullhorn. "She never had a chance."

Louise explains how an egg got stuck in the bird's reproductive tract and caused an infection. "We took her to a vet, but it was too late. She died in the car on the way there. Dora, I'm sorry we couldn't save you."

The emcee is getting more and more agitated. He tries to talk over the protesters, but no one's paying attention. The protesters take turns talking about the animals, and it's starting to feel like a funeral.

Phoebe the lamb, found dead in her stall during another night raid. Olive the octopus, found dead in her tank at an outdoor market. Fuzzy the chick, found in a garbage bin together with hundreds of his brothers.

"Fuzzy, I'm sorry we couldn't save you," says the young woman in jeans at one end of the V. She strokes the chick gently, and then the protesters begin to chant.

"They deserve better," one says with conviction.

"No more slaughter," says another.

They speak one by one, and then in unison. "They deserve better. They're our friends. They wanted to live!"

"You're being totally disrespectful!" barks the emcee. "This is a private meeting. Now get out of here or we'll call the police."

The protesters still aren't acknowledging him. They keep chanting and the woman from the pork board gets out of her chair, which is off to one side of the stage. And then she does something— what's she doing? I can't believe it. She's up on the stage with the protesters. She's chanting along with them. That's when it occurs to me to do the same thing.

"They wanted to live!" I say. And soon, others join in. By the time Louise closes the protest, by the time the activists leave to take the animals to a crematorium across town, everyone in the room is on the same side. Some people are crying, some are hugging each other, and some have approached the protesters asking to pet the animals as if they were dogs or cats.

Only the emcee and a handful of organizers have walked out and stand scowling in the hallway, debating whether to call the police or wait it out to avoid unwanted publicity. The emcee is yelling into his cell phone, and I know he's talking to Pim.

A few minutes later, I leave the auditorium rehearsing what I'll say tomorrow at the welfare office. I've dreaded this day since the beginning. Now that it's finally here, it's really not so bad.

***

Spring 2012.

I came to the university this morning with Quigley. But it's Tansy, my supervisor in the mailroom, who drives me back to the office in the afternoon. In a few minutes, I assume, Tansy is the one who will escort me out the door.

"Pim is livid," Tansy finally says after a quiet car trip and a quiet walk down the hall to the mailroom. "Livid! What were you thinking?"

But she cuts me off before I can answer. "Quigley just walked out on us after thirty-three years. Can you imagine how that looks? The senior kindness emissary, protesting an event he helped organize!

"You're not irreplaceable, Moose. No one is. Pim asked me to tell you that if you ever think about pulling something like this again, you will be terminated. You're on probation. Sorry, Moose, but that's what he asked me to say."

Probation? That's it? I want to laugh. "Can I go?"

"Not yet," she says. "There's more. We're in a crisis. Someone from the shelter did a stupid thing and leaked information to the media. We're getting calls every five minutes about the ringworm outbreak."

Ringworm outbreak? "What ringworm outbreak?"

"Haven't you heard?" she asks. "Well, only a few people knew about it before yesterday. I just found out yesterday. The shelter has to put all the animals down because of a super-virulent strain of ringworm that won't go away."

"All the animals? Why?"

"Because the fungus just won't go away," she repeats, as if she's talking to a slow child. "They have to do what they call a . . . a depopulation. Then they have to scrub and bleach every surface, every square inch of the place, after the building is empty."

"There must be some other way," I say. "Foster care—"

"There's no other way," she says. "They've tried everything else. Everything that's responsible. If they send an animal with ringworm to a foster home and a child catches it, or an old person—"

"But—"

"Look," she says. "I don't like it either, but we can't question this decision. Three senior employees have walked out over the past two days. And you're in enough trouble over that protest today."

"Well—"

"Pim wants you to go on Predation tomorrow morning and explain this decision."

It's not funny, but I'm fighting a freakish impulse to laugh. I've watched the show, of course: Predation has topped the prime-time ratings for three years straight. It pits friends and family members against each other, usually over some contentious social or political issue. They take turns baiting until one person can't take it anymore. On every show, the guest representing the more popular side dresses up as a predatory animal. So far they've had Superlion, Super-T.-rex, Viperella, and I don't know how many others.

"You mean defend it?" I ask Tansy.

"Explain it," she says. "Why it's best for the community, for public health. Other animals in the community. Other animals this shelter could help, who won't get our help if we have to spend the next six months on lockdown."

Predation.

My mind jumps to the Barricudaman episode. Last year the ratings shot way up after a guest died under suspicious circumstances only a few days after facing Barracudaman. I'm wracking my brain now, but I can't remember what the controversy was and whether the dead man won or lost. And then I remember the shelter animals and feel bad for letting my mind wander.

"They invited us," Tansy says, frowning at my expression. "Pim thinks it's a chance to give our side."

"Then why doesn't he do the show? Why does it have to be me?"

"I can't tell you why," Tansy says, shaking her head. "Sorry. It's complicated."

***

Spring 2012.

Standing backstage with a blue folder in my hands, I'm staring at three pages of typed point-form notes. Inane soundbites written by a staff vet and edited by Pim. I've rehearsed my lines; all I have to do is say them. Now I stare out at the harsh studio lights, take a breath, and get ready to face Louise.

She's standing center stage, flanked by two younger activists, wearing the same Bastet T-shirt she had on yesterday over the same bottle-green leotard and tights. The young activists, a man and a woman, are both in jeans.

Louise started wearing factory goggles a few years ago instead of sunglasses. The woman at her side replaces the goggles with a Baroque mask made of handcrafted black and green paper feathers, decorated with gold trim and shiny black beads. The papier mâché beak is black and bright yellow.

The young man takes a black cape out of a box and hands it to the young woman, who helps Louise put it on. Next is a pair of wings made of black and gold lamé fabric. The wings are much taller than Louise, but only a little taller than the two young activists, who fasten them to her torso and buckle them in place before carefully adjusting her cape.

Finally, the young man takes out a pair of yellow plush talons. They're about the size of boxing gloves. He hands one to the young woman, and together they hold them out so Louise can slip her hands in.

The young man picks up the box. He and the young woman salute Louise, then turn and walk off the set in opposite directions. The audience cheers as Louise raises her talons.

My powder-blue dress came from a thrift store last year, but it looked new this morning. I thought I was ready for this, but all of a sudden I can feel the floor drop out from under my feet. I'm underdressed, I realize now. Underdressed and unprepared.

The audience boos as I enter the stage, and someone throws a slimy brown banana peel. It misses my face but grazes my foot, as I take my seat on a mint-green couch that nearly matches Louise's hair.

The production manager motions to Louise to sit next to me. She declines, preferring to stand.

Jessica Barksdale

Costumes

"His mom runs a rodeo," her best friend Dana said from her nest of clothes and blankets on Susan's full-sized bed. She was waiting for Susan to get dressed, so they could meet up with Dana's boyfriend Charles and the new guy at school, Anthony.

"Does he ride a horse?"

"Aren't there bulls at a rodeo?" Dana stared at her phone screen, tapping at things with one finger.

"Who cares what animal!" Susan said. "Can you say rodeo? Aren't they illegal now?"

Dana ignored her.

"Isn't it an instance of animal cruelty?"

Dana shrugged.

Couldn't anyone see he was untrustworthy with his rodeo, his three cell phones and no socks, a boy who teased—that's what he did to Susan today about her shirt.

"What color is that?" He'd mock-shielded his eyes from the terrible glare.

But, really, who could blame him? Her shirt was horrid, short-sleeved, and worse, puce.

"I don't have anything to wear," Susan said, plucking at her shirt.

"God, what a color. Either puce or rotten purple," Dana said, voice muffled. "Fact is, you should throw it away like yesterday."

"So why does he want me to be there anyway?" Susan asked.

Dana looked up from her phone, her face an eerie blue.

"He likes you," Dana said and then went back to tapping, her perfect black nails clacking on the screen.

Dana was dressed all in black, as if she wanted to steal expensive paintings from museums or partner up with Batman. But with her dark hair and huge black eyes, she was a fully matching set, mysterious and thin, able to slip into cracks and hide.

Susan, on the other hand, wore the ugly shirt and a pair of ripped jeans and her old Converse. Her hair wasn't blonde or brown but a fine wild flurry of in-between. The past year or two, she hadn't bothered thinking about what she wore, focusing on school and Dana, who was now otherwise occupied with Charles.

She sighed, the air that escaped her heavy, as though she'd breathed it in a year ago. Going shopping now wasn't an option. Her mother's closet wouldn't help Susan either—filled with crap with spangles and even bells, as if she was a reindeer or a Christmas tree.

"Find something that shows him who you are," Dana said, now texting someone, probably Charles.

"Fine." Kicking at her castoff clothes, Susan dug through her top drawer. Last summer, she bought a T-shirt with one word on it: Memory.

Some word. She needed another, and said out loud, "Poem."

"Quixotic," Dana said, she with the one million on her SATs. She had to get something out of all that studying.

Rather than search for anything else to wear, Susan opened her bedroom door, left Dana on the bed, and headed to the kitchen for some of the chicken her mother made three days ago, just before going out with Joey, that idiot she met at the Marriott in Sacramento.

But the refrigerator smelled so lonely, she shut it and ended up in the garage, standing next to the graveyard of old Halloween costumes: princess, ghost, witch, roller derby queen. There, she flicked through them all, admiring a sparkly princess mask, a ballerina tutu, and a witch hat. Apparently, she'd never been a cowgirl, which might have been useful now, Anthony and his mom all about cows.

The yellow garage light flickered, the sparkles in the outfits glittering like tiny specks of costume jewelry. For some reason, her mother had kept every costume, from the stretchy pumpkin onesie to Susan's last trick-o-treating in eighth grade: Hermione Granger— a dirty blonde wig, black cape, never-ending bag, and magic wand. Here hung the only evidence of Susan's childhood, her mother refusing to put up photographs in the house—not on her dresser, not on the walls.

"Dates won't believe I'm thirty-two if they see you around?" her mother had said.

Her mother was forty-four and wore pants so tight they left deep red welts when she took them off. She rubbed creams and other potions on the backs of her hands and pulled her ponytail tight to get rid of her tiny crow's feet. She only ate grapefruit and popcorn and celery.

"Don't come home tonight," her mother often said.

Or, "I'm not coming home tonight."

As of right now, Susan hadn't seen her mother since the chicken night. An empty pain beat hot and sad under her ugly puce shirt. She was alone, with no evidence of her life on this planet except costumes. Too bad she'd never been an astronaut, able to live on the moon. Or Mars.

The stiff, cheap fabrics rustled under her hand. Forget shopping, her mother, or trying to look good. Forget about Dana's standards. Susan was going to go with weird. Very weird. Weird as weird could be, and she was weird, enough that she'd said yes to Anthony in the first place. Enough that she didn't have a past or anyone who really cared about her.

Maybe she was lucky that a boy she didn't really know wanted to hang out with her. She barely deserved it.

"Xenophobic," Dana had said when Susan complained about Anthony's sparse black mustache and baggy pants.

Yet, he was different and had been other places, new enough to town that he could hang with a princess witch ballerina with Hermione hair. Maybe he was a boy who could handle it, her, all of it, cocking his head, taking her in.

"Hi," he'd say. "Wow."

"Take my picture," she would say, posing for his phone.

Susan would take that photo, print it out, and put it on the living room mantle, on the walls, and in her mother's room.

Pulling items off the rack, Susan put on the Hermione wig, the witch hat, the black cape and turned back toward the house, ready now for her first date.

Karen George

Ripping Off the Bandage

I wondered if my friend Glenna would show at Rizzo's. We'd planned our lunch at the beginning of our phone conversation the previous night. By the time I hung up the phone, my neck and shoulders felt so tight I needed a glass of honey bourbon to relax enough to sleep.

She was already fifteen minutes late, but I'd grown accustomed to that over the years, chose to accept it as my opportunity to learn patience. We'd known each other since grade school. Fifteen years ago, she'd moved five states away for her husband's job, and returned a year ago when they ended their twenty-year marriage.

My husband Arlen and I frequented Rizzo's Italian Grille for ten years, and after his death three years ago, I ate here at least once a week. I felt close to him here.

Arrangements of old black-and-white photos covered the restaurant walls from eye level to near the ceiling—different sizes, some frames ornate gold and silver, others unadorned. Singular subjects and family groups—marriages, graduations, reunions, funerals. The walls also held framed mirrors, a picture or two of a Madonna and child, and movie stars such as Sophia Loren, Gina Lollobrigida, and Virna Lisi.

When seated at the table Arlen and I regularly occupied, I spotted an odd space on the wall across from me. Instead of a framed photo, a tiny blank Post-it note hung in the middle of the 5x7 spot that was cleaner than the rest of the wall.

Had one of the tall young busboys caught the frame with their shoulder, knocked it down, broke it? Maybe the owner or manager hadn't gotten around to repairing it. I remembered the missing photo displayed a dark-haired woman in her late teens to early twenties wearing a satin V-neck swing dress I imagined as emerald. Seated on a couch covered in a large exotic plant fabric that matched the drapes, she wore shiny earrings and a necklace, a magnolia pinned in wavy hair near her ear. She looked like my mother in her engagement picture.

I wondered if the woman and owner had a falling out, and if so, why not hang another photo in its place, instead of leaving that miniature Post-it note with the edges curled up? Maybe intended as a bookmark, a placeholder, saying, Remember the woman here? Forget her.

I ordered a glass of water with lemon; told the young man I was waiting for someone to join me.

The hostess seated two men at the table beneath the missing picture. Both wore burgundy cordovan leather oxfords. A blonde with tortoiseshell-framed glasses faced me, dressed in navy chinos with a red, tan, and green plaid cotton button-down. The man with his back to me had a long ponytail—black streaked with silver. He wore a charcoal-gray dress shirt. His elbows on the table pulled the fabric, which looked like silk, across his shoulder blades. When Arlen wore silk, I couldn't stop touching him.

I could hear the men's conversation. The blonde talked about a visit with his uncle as he died. The blonde's voice held such reverence and gratitude, it reminded me of witnessing my father's death—how uncomfortable I felt while also privileged to be there. Arlen died in his sleep while out of town on business.

I speculated about the relationship of these two lunching together. As they talked, I learned they were business associates. The ponytailed man owned the company where the blonde worked.

A few overheard phrases revealed the business sold computer software. My occasional view of the black-haired man's hands led me to imagine him an artist or an art therapist. I could feel his fingers on my skin. It surprised me to be thinking of a man in a sexual way. I hadn't desired anyone since Arlen's death, had grown to love living alone.

The click of high heels on tile floor made me turn to see Glenna approaching with a warm smile—nothing to indicate anything lingering from our conversation the previous night. She wore a white lace-edged tank top tucked into black straight-leg jeans cinched with a silver studded leather belt. She'd lost even more weight since we'd met a month ago.

The blonde watched her walk toward me. I'd tell her later how much he'd appreciated what he'd seen. She'd gone through a bad time when she found out her husband cheated on her throughout their marriage.

I rose to hug her, not detecting any stiffness on her part. I hoped my body hadn't conveyed any tension.

***

Right before we'd hung up the phones last night, I double-checked the time we agreed to meet, and Glenna said that gave her enough time to get to Clayton's department store to buy a gift for her niece's baby shower before we met for lunch, and enough time before her two o'clock appointment for what she called her cut and color.

I'm not sure why I mentioned boycotting Clayton's because they didn't support LGBTQ rights.

"That's precisely why I go there," she said.

I thought I had heard her wrong, but her sarcastic tone spoke volumes. My cheeks burned. I couldn't believe that someone I'd known and loved for so many years didn't support gay and trans rights.

An uneasy silence had fallen. I'd finally said, "See you tomorrow. Love you," and hung up before she could reply.

"Been waiting long?" Glenna asked.

"No, I just got here," I lied. "You look great."

Her medium length, layered strawberry-blond hair framed her face. Earrings swayed when she moved. Their silver-blue gemstones matched the color of her irises.

"I ought to. I'm beating my brains out exercising every day."

"Well, it definitely paid off." I leaned close, whispered, "That blonde man at the table across from us can't keep his eyes off you."

She grinned, raised her brows.

The waiter brought a loaf of crusty bread, poured a puddle of olive oil in a small, shallow bowl, added a few drops of balsamic vinegar, and some fresh-ground pepper. I tore off a hunk, asked if she'd found a present for her niece.

Her gaze fell to the dish. She dipped a piece of bread, as she described the onesie and matching blanket she'd found. Her eyes met mine for a second before dropping again, her cheeks flushed.

I felt like I held my breath. It maddened and saddened me how nervous we were with each other. Surely we weren't going to let a differing opinion mess up our friendship. I tried to draw her into neutral topics of conversation, but she resisted joining. Maybe the awkward silence between us represented a waypost, and we needed to revisit it to move pass it.

I glanced again at the tiny Post-it note on the wall where the dark-haired woman's photo once hung.

After we gave the waiter our food orders, I took a gulp of my wine, and leaned close to tell her to check out the ponytailed man in the silk shirt. "Wouldn't you like to get your hands in his hair?"

Her look of appreciation turned sad. I realized the man's hair resembled her ex-husband's.

"I forgot to tell you something last night." Her eyes widened, lips formed a wicked grin. "My former sister-in-law Shelley told me Stan no longer lives with the woman he left me for. She believes he's going to call me."

I didn't know how to respond. My silence heavied the air. Would Stan call Glenna, and would she take him back? I replied with a noncommittal, "hmm." She looked disappointed I didn't rally her side, or say she deserved more than her ex-husband.

Our food arrived—my Wild Mushroom Ravioli, her Tomato Caprese.

"How's your quilting coming?" I asked. She crafted exquisite, prizewinning quilts and wall hangings.

"I'm not really quilting anymore."

"Oh, no," I replied without thinking. "You do such beautiful work. I still display your pinwheel, postage stamp, and double wedding ring quilts." I knew only too well how shame corrodes your life.

"Well, quilting's really out of fashion. No one wants them. I'm just not inspired anymore."

"Well, you've been through hell."

After Arlen died, I didn't make pottery for a year. When I started again, I never stopped.

Glenna had barely touched her food.

"How's your Caprese?" I asked.

"Good. I'm just not very hungry."

When the waiter returned, we asked him to box up our meals. I could easily finish mine but felt awkward wolfing it down while she picked at hers.

"I'm thinking of taking up watercolor painting," she said.

For a second her smile brought back the friend of my youth—the one who skydived with me as a college graduation gift to ourselves; who joined me sneaking out of our houses at night to meet guys at the drive-in; who skinny-dipped with me in the ocean; visited a nudist colony with me. When had she turned so conservative?

"Would you take a class with me?" she asked.

"Oh my god, yes, I'd love to. Always thought that I'd go for that medium when we were in art school, but then I chose pottery to concentrate on. Find out what classes are available and let me know." I raised my glass of wine. "Let's toast to new ventures."

We tapped glasses, but her smile faded. She looked at her fingernails painted a shimmery pink.

"Your nails are beautiful." I'd given up coloring mine after Arlen died.

"I treated myself to a manicure."

Glenna stared into my eyes "Cindy, what do you think I should do if Stan calls?"

She sounded so hopeful. I took a deep breath. "I can't see any harm in talking to him, if you feel like it."

"But what if he asks if I'll take him back?"

"Um, that's a hard one."

"I know. I don't even know if he'll call." Her voice wavered. "But I need to be prepared, have an answer ready if he calls and asks."

I made a spur of the moment decision to reveal something I'd never told another person. When Arlen died, I decided no one ever needed to know it. Let my humiliation die with him. I didn't need to carry it any longer. But of course I still did.

"I don't think there's a right or wrong answer, Glenna. It's whatever you feel in your heart. You might decide no way, and then when he asks, you might feel why the hell not?"

I shared that Arlen cheated on me. I could have claimed it happened to a friend, but it felt right to admit the truth to my lifelong friend, no matter how uncomfortable. So many times I'd longed to tell Glenna, especially after she revealed her husband's infidelity. But I felt so much shame and doubt about sticking with my marriage.

"I didn't think I could ever forgive him, or trust him again. People make mistakes, and sometimes they learn from them. He swore he loved me, and I still loved him. It sounds like a cliché, something you see in every silly TV soap opera. I decided to take a chance, hope we could get past it, and be happy again. It wasn't easy, but I grew to love him on a much deeper level."

I finished off my wine. "You know it broke my heart when you and Stan divorced."

"Oh honey." Glenna leaned toward me, touched my hand. "I wish you told me about Arlen's affair, and I wish I stayed with you for a while after his funeral. I just didn't know what to do."

"What we should do now is order a stiffer drink," I insisted, "Or else we're both going to start bawling."

"Let's get a honey bourbon and a cinnamon whiskey. We'll share, like the old days."

"Okay. I don't have cooties. Do you?"

We both laughed. Our drinks arrived, and after a few sips of each, Glenna's face turned serious.

"There's a favor I want to ask you. It's something really important to me. I'm a little afraid to do it by myself. It's something I've never done."

The hairs rose on my arms.

"You know how much I've wanted children." Her voice trembled.

I nodded, remembering past conversations. When friends and family inquired about when I might have children, I avoided answering. It was none of their business that Arlen and I chose not to.

"I deeply regret that I never convinced Stan to go to the infertility specialist, or consider adoption."

She took a big swig of the cinnamon whiskey. "St. Brigit's is sponsoring a Right to Life rally Sunday. They're making a human chain against abortion on the Suspension Bridge." She took a deep breath. "They've asked us to recruit a friend. Will you go with me?" Before I could answer, she continued. "You know, I've never been in a protest, and I'm nervous, but if you were there."

Her words came faster, louder, and higher pitched. "We plan to block traffic. I could wind up in jail." Both hands on the table, she tilted toward me.

I touched her fingertips.

She rifled through details of the protest. I half-listened, scrambling for words to refuse her request. I could have lied, alleged I'd made plans with my sister. My attention drifted to the wall where the Post-it clung. I realized that as much as I wanted to know the truth behind the missing photo, it wasn't the truth I needed to claim.

"Glenna." I waited for her to meet my gaze. "I'm sorry I can't support you. I'm not going to pretend to believe in something I don't."

Her eyes opened wide. "You mean to tell me you believe in killing babies?"

The venom in her voice stunned me. The men seated at the table under the Post-it note side-glanced our way. I imagined the restaurant owner snatching the woman's photo off the wall.

"I can't say I'm for or against abortion. It'd be a hard decision to make, and I'm glad I never faced the need to. But I do believe it should be a woman's choice to resolve, not—"

I restrained from saying what I wanted to—the issue sure as hell didn't belong in the hands of Catholic priests or bishops or the Pope—men who'd abused children and/or hid that fact for years.

"Hasn't the Catholic Church and other fundamental religions shit on women enough already?" I asked in as calm a tone as I could manage.

She pushed her chair away from the table, a loud scrape.

I pinched my thigh between my thumb and forefinger, took a breath. "It's a complicated subject. All I can do is respect your opinion, and hope you'll respect mine."

Her face relaxed a little.

For years, I'd kept such opinions to myself, avoided conflict at any cost, which resulted in others assuming I believed the same as them. I'd finally begun to see that as cowardice on my part.

"What's happened to you?" Glenna asked, forehead scrunched.

"I could ask you the same question. I'm tired of keeping my beliefs hidden so as not to hurt other peoples' feelings. If I can't be truthful with my best friend, why have a best friend?"

She closed her eyes, shook her head no.

I waited for her to speak, finished off the honey bourbon, thankful for the warmth radiating through me.

The waiter dropped off our checks. "No hurry. Take your time. We're slow today."

We pulled our shoulder bags off the back of our chairs, rummaged for wallets, extracted credit cards, slid them between the leather slit. I placed my envelope on the table between us. She set hers beside mine, drank the remaining cinnamon whiskey, stared past me across the room.

I broke the silence when we rose to leave. "Let me know about the watercolor class. It sounds wonderful."

Glenna nodded, unveiled the hint of a smile before she turned for the exit

Robert Pope

The Metal Detector

My ninth-grade English teacher just moved to our burg and had names of students from her previous school, wonderful young men and women, curious and of good character. If anyone would like to correspond in real letters with any of them, see her. After class, Mrs. Fisk gave me the card with Alex's name and address. "You'll like Alex," she said, smiling as if she knew something I didn't. We wrote to each other all the way through eleventh grade. He was a year ahead, graduated and started working as a groundskeeper for a country club golf course. He and his dad came here for the fishing fairly regularly, once a year, until his dad died.

The name of the cabins stuck in my mind because it was a bird that rarely frequented my own region. Once you have the name, you can find anything or anywhere in the world online. But the thing I liked about these particular cabins: no online service, which meant no one could spy on or hack me for a couple of weeks. I got so cavalier, I worked out in the open, alternately sitting at my picnic table and in a faux Adirondack with wide arm rests across which my slab of board served as a writing desk.

Tuesday, second week, after a solid week of wheel spinning, I sat out in my faux desk in sandals, shorts, T-shirt (light yellow with a picture of a lemon front and center), and a layer of sunblock over my forehead and nose and cheeks and the back of my neck. This does not include a baseball cap with an Oriole on the front—in honor of my erstwhile pen pal, who, last I checked on him, was a groundskeeper at Camden Yards. By the way, I do not live in Baltimore or in Maryland. Every once in a while, the scent of wet, burnt logs came to me from a large, iron tractor wheel fire pit. First real day of work. Five paragraphs deep and hot to trot.

I brought my kayak with me so whenever I couldn't write the next word, I took off down the river with a sandwich and a short-handled fishing rod. It got so I wasn't sure whether I went kayaking to avoid or because I could not do any work. Unsurprisingly, no one showed up to impede my progress and I worked right through to dusk, much of it usable in this or another form. I have to get it down before I can shape or edit. I need to see what it looks like before I know what it ought to look like. I never know what it ought to look like until it's done.

I generally write about local real estate and politics, an enormous bore until I discovered a little racket connecting them in unusual ways. I had done the research, found the disgruntled witnesses, and definitely did not keep notes on my computer or send info through text or email. I kept my private notebooks under lock and key and written in a code my teenage pen pal and I developed—or thought we developed—for our secret letters and kept them in my briefcase under lock and key. It wasn't that I didn't care to be scooped; these people had gotten in deep.

This was early June, weather varying between sun and rain and wind, all weather reports useless—chilly in the morning and at night in the forest with the river wandering past and only three other cabins spread out along the bank. The caretaker lived in number one, and I had the second cabin, nice space between us. Nothing on the other side of the river but trees—pine with assorted hardwoods—birds and deer and acres and acres of bugs of all sorts. At least I could be certain there were no personal bugs in the cabins, by which I mean listening devices.

One thing I should add here about the code. I could read it like regular English, write it as well as I knew my own name and address. We kept it up for several years, until, as I say, he got the groundskeeper job. We might have gotten the code off a television show or from a book on codes, a subject of interest at the time. We thought it was ours alone.

You make a key by drawing in four grids, two on top, two below. A tic-tac-toe grid for the first and another where you cross two lines so they meet in the center and end up with four triangles. Below this, repeat the same designs but with a dot in each of the nine openings in the first grid and the four in the second; the diamond grid, I call it. Starting at the top of the first grid, put an alphabet letter in each of the openings moving by rows for the first grid and from the top clockwise for the second. Simple, but who knew? You'd have to have a serious interest in a document to waste your time decoding it.

Alex told me the most banal details of his day, I told him mine. We did a lot of supposing and guessing and laughing, as I recall. I kept all his letters in a shoe box, and he did the same with mine. Once I found my mother in my bedroom looking through the letters, several lying open on my bed, another in her hand. When she turned to look at me she seemed to be wondering whether her only child was a spy, stupid, or batshit crazy. She threw the last one on the bed and swept out in a blaze of blue dress and lilac. She never asked what they were.

The work went well Wednesday. I did not touch the kayak. The caretaker came by and asked if I needed more firewood. It was almost comical the way he kept calling me Jake. This was my fake ID from high school. I used it when I didn't want anyone to know where I was, like this time. My name on the ID was Jake Boynton. I'd successfully gotten drunk as Jake Boynton, and now I registered under the same name, as if Jake had finally grown up and made his reappearance in the world. The caretaker was a man in his sixties, I'd guess, with clipped white hair and a reddish cast to his face and significant freckling.

It never surprised me that he went about bare chested. His chest looked about like his face, with a generous sprinkling of white curls. A person interesting to me for the simple fact of his existence. I knew he did not drink nor take substances to while away the dull hours. I carried on a brief conversation with him, friendly, but I was not actually present for the performance.

He was no disturbance. That's what I liked about him. I was in this trance, clicking away, knocking the hell out of the piece when I heard an odd beep I could not for the life of me identify. Three times in a row, in relatively rapid succession. In the next cabin was this stout gentleman (none of it jiggled) who never said a word that I heard. I wondered how he made his bread, but I was pretty sure it hadn't come from him. He was at that moment sitting on his porch facing the river doing something on his smart phone, which must have had its own internet hookup.

I get nervous around quiet people, like me. I dress and groom myself to pass undetected through life as much as possible with so many tics I can never (evidently) fully hide all of them. This fellow was monotone. Pale peach shirt, light tan shorts, white socks and shoes, oddly agile for his size. I had seen him sprint to his car, a black Mercedes. He didn't have a problem getting where he wanted to go. I do not take anyone for granted, that's a fact. I am not a wonderfully trusting lad. I give no trouble where I've gotten none, but don't get on my bad side. It makes me wonder what you're up to. At work, they call me The Wasp.

That's what kept me typing away beside the river rather than some nice fellow who didn't want to get his oxford smirched. That's probably why I go through so many people and try to make it up with thoughtful gifts. That's a category I keep. For people who have been interviewed by my mildly brutalizing style. I get the results, not him. If I be waspish best beware my sting. I'm not the kind of person who needs crowds hanging on my lapels. Just a few friends I can go to when my reserves of fellow-feeling require restoration. For more important things, I turn to my former girlfriend Lisa, who remains my closest confidant.

When the beeps continued sporadically, I got up, walked past the bushes separating my site from my neighbor's (an agent perhaps hired by the turdballs stinking up our city) so I could look way down the path to cabin four the other side of Danger Mouse; there I saw a fellow in an open short-sleeve blue shirt and faded jeans, bare-foot unless I missed my guess, scouring the ground in front of his cabin with a metal detector. When he got a beep, he kneeled and dug at the dirt with some kind of hand spade. He turned the dirt and then stood and hovered the thing over the ground until the next beep, whereupon the performance repeated itself ad nauseam as if he were some pointless machine created in Nature's spare time and forgotten, left here to this thankless task. I almost felt sorry for him.

He had a vendetta against his front yard. I hoped he might dig up a working watch so he'd know how much time he wasted at this occupation. I couldn't work the rest of the day for that wretchedly ignorant beeping. It had no purpose other than to alert Mr. Blue to the presence of the bent and blackened fork he held up to his eye as if it were a precious gem. I wanted to crawl out of my skin. I went out on my kayak for an hour or two, and by the time I pulled it up on my little section of the shore, I had concocted a plan that I would sneak into his cabin while he was out, if he ever went out, and find a way to disable the device. Lacking that, break it. If not break then steal.

I took the path, passed the Agent's cabin, and there he was, running that imaginary flying saucer on a stick over the side yard now. It infuriated me. I went inside, thinking he would probably have covered his entire yard by the next day, so I poured myself a scotch and whiled away the evening lying back on the couch with my head on the arm and the cold glass on my sternum, completely at peace. I laughed aloud when I remembered that knucklehead hoping to find a quarter or a bobby pin or a metal button so hard he swept the entire front yard.

Next day, silence. Birds. Water. Gentle lapping. Occasional hum of an insect. And the tap, tap, tapping of my laptop, translating braille into sausages. Two in the afternoon, on the nose. Beep. Beep, beep. I left my computer on the picnic table by the cabin and crept past the bush. Nothing. When I heard him again, he sounded more distant. Hmmn, I hummed to myself. Hmmn. I hurried past the neighbor's cabin the other way, toward the water, held onto a skinny tree so I could stretch my neck out to see him working in the backyard. It occurred to me he had been a squirrel in a former life, still searching for his nuts. The only nuts were in his head.

Maybe mine as well. It got in my head and I couldn't get it out. I'd sit down, get back to the words, and be going fine when here it came: beep. During the pauses I could see in my mind's eye that he would be kneeling obediently beside the apparatus and digging with his little hand spade. If the owner had any grass seed, this might be an optimum time for planting. But hanging on that tree as much as I did gave me to know he too had a kayak, even though I had never seen him on the water. If he ever did, I'd be watching and hightail it around the back, where the bank rose to a hillock. I'd be virtually hidden to The Agent should he be looking my way.

What would happen then, I left unplanned. I didn't want to think I'd actually do anything until he started in on the near side yard. It was almost worse that I couldn't see him, blocked by the Agent's cabin. I could hear him and I could see him in my mind. I eked out a few paragraphs of labored lines, tugged against the wind by the Volga Boatman. Through it all, beep, beep, dig. I had thought I could wrap this up in a month, but not at this rate. Because of that nitwit with the metal detector. Then came the breakthrough. While hanging on the tree at dusk, I noticed straight-away the kayak was no longer where it had been every single day, which meant, most likely, the hunter for worthless treasures had finally taken her out.

Without another thought, I dropped down to the bank and slinked along the hill, bent over just in case. I climbed back up where the bank became steepest by holding to the roots of a tree. I skinned my knees up a bit, no blood. A little shakier, I crouched behind the cabin, looking for an open window or a door. It had gotten a bit darker, difficult to see details clearly, but I did find a side door propped open with a stone, for the air. There was a screen door that could be shut with a hook and eye latch. I realized with a lurch in my heart that his car, some kind of SUV, had the kayak fastened to the roof. Hmmn.

The screen, it turned out, had not been latched, so I peeked into what passed for a living room into the darkness. There he was, asleep on a couch wearing nothing but a pair of white briefs, one foot on the floor. His mouth had fallen open and his eyes completely closed. His breathing came soft and melodious, with a pleasant whistle in his nose. I literally tiptoed into his kitchen, where I found nothing but a half-eaten tuna fish sandwich and a banana peel I could see in what faint light came through a window had turned brown.

I knew a fellow who liked peanut butter and banana sandwiches, but tuna fish and banana seemed unlikely. He had probably eaten them separately, possibly at different times. Banana for breakfast, possibly with cereal. Bowl in the sink, so that's that. Tuna for lunch. I walked quite casually around the brief hallway into the bedroom.

Bed unmade. Nightstand, metal detector rod or handle there against the wall. Shaped a bit like a golf club, an oversized wood made out of metal, the actual detector like a small flying saucer there. I wondered what he saw in this. On top of a chest of drawers a bunch of the doodads he'd dug up, including the famous bent fork of yore.

What made a man do such a thing. I looked around the room and saw a few large plastic tubs with lids and opened one to books and papers and writing implements, some folded terrycloth shirts of varying pastel shades, two pairs of shoes and one of hiking boots, all of it neatly stashed. Interesting contrast to the general lack of attention to detail I detected here and there, a certain number of dishes in the sink, clothes on the end of the bed. Yet in the box, all was orderly.

I lifted out a shoebox, noticing the shoes had been size ten, a couple of sizes smaller than mine. I looked back in the tub to see if it contained the shoes from the box, but it didn't look like it. I heard a noise from the living room and stiffened, attempting to control my breathing. I hurried back to the chest of drawers, grabbed the handle of the detector, and, for some reason, crouched there to avoid detection myself.

I heard him rustling in the kitchen. He had gotten from the couch to the kitchen without my notice, which alarmed me. I didn't know how I would get out if he came into the bedroom. I heard what sounded like grinding coffee beans. It became quite difficult, under these circumstances, to quiet my own breathing. It rattled in my chest and throat—I didn't know how he couldn't hear me. Then he stepped into the bedroom and looked right at me crouched on the floor beside the chest of drawers and the metal detector. He looked at me and for perhaps a minute I couldn't think of what to say. Finally, he broke the ice by asking me what the devil I was doing in his cabin. And why did I have his metal detector in my hands?

When nothing came to me, I said, "I was trying to get some work done when you started beeping with this thing." I stood up, gesturing toward the machine. "Beep, beep, beep," I said. "For what? For these filthy trinkets? I couldn't take it anymore. I couldn't get any writing done. I came here for the peace and quiet."

"You're a writer?"

"A journalist."

"What were you going to do? With the thing?"

"It was driving me crazy, all right? If I couldn't disable it, I was going to take it out in my kayak and drop it where you'd never find it."

He sat down on the edge of the bed and crossed his legs at the knee. "That's intense."

"I've been told I am a bit intense."

I shook my head and looked away from him. "If I thought I could get past you with it, I would still finish what I started. Seriously, what the hell are you doing? What's this all about? It doesn't make any sense. Over and over, beep and dig, beep and dig. For what?"

I had broken into his cabin, sure, but I felt a certain urgency.

"Well," he said at last, "I'm sorry. But you didn't have to break in. You could have told me. You're the guy two cabins down, right?" He leaned over and flicked on the bedside lamp so we could get a good look at each other.

"I don't know," he said. "You don't look very imposing."

"Neither do you, I might point out."

"I've seen you on your laptop out there, in your chair."

"I'm working on something. An exposé, you'd call it. That's why I'm up here, hiding out, so to speak, until I get it done and in my editor's hands. Very hot stuff, to tell the truth."

I realized I had focused on myself perhaps too much, so I asked him what brought him here to the cabins. "I lost something up here. I came back looking for it. A friend gave me the metal detector a while back. He got tired of it. I used to come up here with my Dad," he said. "We'd come fishing." He nodded his head, a bit like a bobblehead doll. "It was the best thing in my life. I looked forward to it all winter, and in the late spring, my Dad and I came up here, going out in the canoe, fishing from the rocks. Cleaning and cooking and eating what we caught and not much else. Talking. Listening to his stories."

"He meant a lot to you."

"He did."

He had gotten himself in a mood. Then he noticed the shoebox where I set it on the bed.

"What's this?" he said. He lifted the lid, and I leaned to see inside. Letters packed in bunches and rows and crosswise. Then he seemed to notice me again. "I won't be running that thing anymore. You're right there. You have me dead to rights. I need to get on. I don't know what I'm looking for anymore."

I knew that hollow feeling in the gut too well. What they didn't tell you, it hurt like hell to be so alone you can't speak to break through. "What are any of us looking for?" I asked him.

"You can leave now," he said.

"Sorry," I said. "Sometimes I'm pretty damned dumb."

He nodded, "That's all right. We've all got too much to think about. Sometimes, I don't know how to go on. I used to reach for something, I can't remember what. Everything good lies in my past." He set his hand on the shoebox. "I'd be grateful if you would leave now."

"Thank you," I said, and hurried past, almost running out the drive to the path back to my place. Panic seized me when I realized I had left my laptop out in the open, where anyone could have seen it. When I glanced at the cabin right beside me, there he was, standing in the grass beside it, looking right at me. That gave me a start. I shouted, "Oh, my God!"

He was wearing a light jacket, maybe tan, light slacks as far as I could tell in the dark. After a pause, he said, without hurry or contrition, "Sorry to have scared you. I came out here to request that you stay to your side of this cabin here, my cabin, the one you've been slinking around, because the next time I catch you I'm going to be a bit more unpleasant." He lifted one side of his jacket to show me the shoulder holster loaded with what appeared to be a snubby, more effective at close range than from a distance.

"Yessir," I said.

"Okay then, get about your own business or get out. Do I make myself clear?"

"You do," I said.

"Keep your door locked the rest of the night. This is for your own safety. Do not open your door for anyone until tomorrow, and then only when you hear my all clear. If you do, it will not go well for you."

"What sign will you give me that it's you? When it's clear."

"I will say, 'All clear.'"

"Is it okay if I drink alcohol?"

"I recommend it."

I went back to my cabin, locked the door, and drank myself into a stupor. I went at it directly and with a purpose. I could not deal with all the confrontation. I was a nervous wreck, which you'll understand. I have been in dangerous situations before, but usually I understood how I got myself there in the first place. It's different when the danger is not of your own making. My nerves were shot to hell.

When I woke in the morning with a not too terrible hangover and only some minor shaking, I drank coffee, moving from one window to the next. I knew nothing of what I had inadvertently stepped in by coming up for some real privacy to write my article. It was thinking like that, actually, that snapped me out of it. I had to get my work done whatever happened, so I put on my work cap and went at it three straight hours, downing two pots of coffee, and by God if I didn't have a draft of the whole thing. I have to give some thanks to Fear. That had me all sparked up.

When I finally came out, it had gotten chilly, so I started a fire in the pit. I had plenty of wood, both kindling and logs, and since I had no paper to ignite, I doused it with lighter fluid. Whoosh it went up. When I turned my back to the heat, I saw flapping from a branch of the bush between cabins an obviously worn sheet of paper that had magically appeared when I had the thought I needed paper, or perhaps it was blown there on a breeze. When I plucked it off, I heard a weird bird call and turned to see a bald eagle sweeping down the river pursued by an angry crow—the kind of thing I see up here on a regular basis. I carried it back to the fire and right before I shoved it in, I glanced at it, struck by the odd markings, obviously not words, but a language of some kind. I held it close, a gesture meant to really look at it, but I knew exactly what it was. My heart made a leap and did a back flip. This guttural shout I had never heard burst out of me. I dropped the paper and literally stepped back from it, all of it involuntary action.

I had gotten too close to the flames again. Before it went up completely, I attempted to fish it out, but no luck. I stood there for a while, staring down into the flames. Something about the way it made me feel called to mind the words mortal terror. I looked around to see if anyone had seen, but, of course, there was no one else there. As I had seen nothing of my nearest neighbor or his Mercedes, I took the path down to my other neighbor's house to see how he had fared. The door was wide open, the screen off its hinges. Inside there was stuff flung all about, mostly garbage, trash, and in the bedroom, the metal detector still stood where I had found it. The plastic bins, the shoebox full of letters, all gone.

One letter must have gotten away from him. Those coded words took flight in order to find me, riding invisible waves of energy that still flowed between Alex and me. I sat on the edge of the bed where Alex sat, and it shook me to my core—what's left of it. That was the only time I ever saw him in my life, and now he's God knows where doing God knows what. It shook me and occasioned if not a dark night, a long night of the soul beside the fire. I actually went down to visit the old man, who I found bare chested again, splitting logs for kindling.

"Hey there, Jake," he said.

"Hey," I said.

"What you know that's good?" He set the ax down to let me know I had his attention.

"Do you know anything about those two?"

He lowered his head waving it back and forth. When he looked up again, he said, "The one fellow come here as a boy. With his dad. Catch them some fish." He put his arm across his forehead to block the sun and watched a lone vulture flapping overhead.

"Did you hear them things screaming last night? Sound almost human, don't they?"

"I must have been sleeping soundly."

"That's one thing folks do here," he said. "That and think." He leaned back a bit from the waist. "I bet you slept a sight better than you do there in the city."

"That I did."

"Anything I can help you with, let me know." He clasped his hands together to signal he needed to get back to splitting. "I have two cabins filling up tomorrow. That one right next to you, with kids. Two of them."

"Well, I wanted to thank you again for your hospitality." I handed him a folded bill (a modest fifty) which he took with a nod I took to mean thanks. "It's been a pleasure getting to know you."

"A pleasure." He had dismissed me, picking up the ax. He glanced back once and I raised a hand. "You're leaving, better scoot. There's a storm coming."

"Thank you," I called back to him.

Sure enough, I saw dark clouds rolling in from a distance. I had to get it through my head whatever happened here wasn't my business. My business was in my laptop ready to go. I packed it up and blew that pop stand. When I got down below to the nearest town, I parked myself at a table in the only coffee shop in town, a well-known hot-wired chain, logged on, and sent a copy of the story to my editor, another to my former girlfriend Lisa.

I heard the crack of lightning and in another moment the rolling thunder. I either had to get back home or lay low until the storm wore off. I could buy a bottle at a liquor store and check into a decent hotel where I could get drunk and have a good cry. But what I did? I called Lisa and hit the road. I'd already done enough crying. Time for The Wasp to sting a few dragons.

Sam Crain

Frank the Dragon

Lei knew better than anyone how hard it was getting started on things. His best friend used to text him every morning to check in and give him encouragement. Logan had been teaching English in a suburb of Beijing. He'd been almost at the end of his two-year stint and Lei had dreaded him going back to the U.S., where he was from. Logan had promised he'd still text, even once they were fourteen hours apart, but Lei was worried it wouldn't be the same.

When Logan died unexpectedly, three weeks before his flight home, Lei didn't have the luxury of being stunned. He had to help— Logan's family had to be told, his things packed up and sent back. They told Lei to find a keepsake to thank him for all his help. Lei kept a small dragon figurine Logan had loved inordinately even though Lei had explained, as gently as he could, that the shop that sold it was infamous for selling claptrap to tourists. He'd been proud of the English word. *At least I didn't get a katana,* Logan had said. *Katana are Japanese*, Lei had replied. *Exactly*, Logan said, setting the little dragon on top of the speaker beside his computer monitor. *His name is Frank.*

Frank rode home in Lei's pocket after everything else—there wasn't all that much—was packed up, Logan's parents' address written in careful English on each box. Lei kept one hand over him, absently stroking the dragon's head with a thumb.

Only once Frank was stationed on Lei's printer did Lei cry for his friend. He palmed the tears from his face, Frank seeming to look at him, and he ached to do something to honor Logan's memory. It had already been eight mornings he'd woken up and gone about his day without the customary text. Of course, his parents had not made Logan an ancestral tablet. Burning joss sticks before Frank would not be the same.

It came to him after a few weeks. The sadness was not a thunderstorm, raining on him with peals of thunder, rattling his ribs. It was like a boulder behind his navel—not precisely in the way but weighing him down, pulling his waist toward his knees, his breastbone to his thighs. But he was not the only one with troubles. His neighbor Yiwei had been struggling with her job, was in danger of missing her deadlines—of disciplinary action. "Blowing it," Logan would have said. Yiwei could get started in the morning, she told Lei, but it seemed like the ability to focus trickled out of her as she ate her lunch. Lei, missing Logan more than ever, had texted Yiwei just after lunchtime: *You can do this!* That done, he returned to his freelance programming assignment.

His phone buzzed twice. *Xiè xiè nǐ* said her text. And she had sent him twelve yuan through WeChat—enough for tea on his next walk, or maybe a snack.

The idea was born painlessly, thrilling to the tips of his fingers, and he'd closed his programming application. He took note of the different things he would need—a way to get clients, a rate scheme, a website.

Frank the Dragon was born: a service Lei marketed as an escape from procrastination and friendlier than a cold, hard deadline. Sometimes, he felt like Logan was sitting just out of his sightline, laughing at the texts he now sent (there was an option for silly jokes) or nodding approvingly at the cute animal photos others chose as rewards. Social media had helped a lot with getting clients. People were overworked, striving to find motivation, and appreciated Lei's willingness to tailor his approach.

It didn't *always* work. Sometimes, he struck the wrong tone. *I have faith you will achieve*, he texted to a new client.

What the hell do you know? the client texted back. *I don't need your faith.*

I am sorry. Would you like a different kind of affirmation? Our kitten photos are very popular.

No. Fuck off!

Lei's phone buzzed in his hand with the profane reply and his hands shook a little. His eyes sought Frank, and for a moment, he felt Logan's hand on his shoulder. *No one can read everyone.* Logan had told him that once, speaking from experience with a father who thought teaching English abroad for so little money was a waste of time. Logan had once confessed that Lei felt more like a brother to him than his actual brother at home, who was finishing up high school. Lei had blushed hot at this admission—one no one else he knew would ever make. Now, he took gulping breaths, trying *not* to think Logan's father might have been right.

No. It was an aneurysm. Logan could have had that anywhere. Being here did not kill him.

In through the nose, out through the mouth. It had already been eight minutes. He was alone again in his room, with Frank gazing unblinking from his perch.

I am sorry again, Lei typed, and he pasted the Refund link into the message. Setting his phone down, he went to wash his face. He needed air.

In a few months, Lei was programming less, which was a bit of a relief, and he made a decent living even if his mother didn't quite understand what he was doing. She only shook her head when he tried to explain.

The anniversary of Logan's death was getting close and the grief-stone was getting heavy again, and Lei found himself wishing as he brushed his teeth and got dressed that *he* had someone to text him. He had indeed honored the spirit of Logan's generosity but there was still no one to do it for him.

He nearly hit himself on the forehead over his breakfast at thinking he could be the only person to think of this idea—what Americans online sometimes called the "mom friend override." A few minutes' search revealed a website not so different from his. He wondered which of them had unintentionally copied the other. Then he decided he'd better have a fake name.

Into the Contact Form he typed for name Ha Jin—it was an author Logan had liked but who wrote in English, so hopefully the website person wouldn't notice. For *Area of Difficulty* he put "getting started" and chose "friendly text" as his intervention option. It would cost him ten yuan a day after his week's free trial.

He'd selected the encouragement in English option, but by day three he was half-regretting it: a facsimile of Logan's texts was not Logan, though he did feel close to his friend when he texted others in the strongly idiomatic English he'd picked up during their friendship.

On day four, he wrote to his coach, asking to switch to Mandarin texts, please. The text on day four brought equal parts regret and relief, and it did spur him to start his own work. It was easier with the Mandarin texts. A handful of times, Lei considered opting back to English but decided against it—it would have been a form of denial, an attempt to pretend Logan himself was still there: surely a dangerous indulgence.

A full month, and Lei was wondering if the texts from his anti-procrastination coach were getting friendlier, more personal. They'd certainly gotten longer.

Another month, and his coach had started adding GIFs even though they were supposed to cost extra, waving aside Lei's offer to pay the proper rate for them.

He was nearly done with a day's work when his phone buzzed. It was his coach. *I'm off the clock. Want to get a coffee or tea?*

Yes, he replied. T*omorrow afternoon? I know a place.* He typed in the address.

I'll be wearing red, she replied.

I'll be in the duck shirt. It was a nod to one of their GIFs.

The date made, Lei realized he didn't know his coach's name or gender, had assumed the "she." There was no reason to feel so nervous about this, he told himself as he combed his hair over again and caught sight of Frank as he crossed to his desk for his phone. It was one-fifteen. At two he had to remember to text a few clients. Hopefully his coach would understand—who better? But what if his coach thought him a fraud for passing himself off as a coach, but needing one himself? His stomach knotted and he worked to ignore it.

The blouse was crimson and shiny, catching the light and returning it.

"I am Yang Lei," he said, seeing no other red shirts in the café.

"Zheng An." She smiled at him.

They were sharing a pot of tea and some steamed buns. By the time they had eaten a bun each, it was two o'clock and Zheng An wanted to know what he, Lei, did. "Please excuse me," Lei said, taking out his phone and texting in English, "I'm sure you're doing great today" to the client who would be expecting it. He pressed SEND.

Zheng An's phone chimed. They looked down then back at Lei. "Wait. *You're* Frank the Dragon?"

"Yes."

Impossible to say which of them was blushing more intensely. "I—promise I did not copy your business," Lei said, keeping his eyes on the basket of buns that still steamed faintly. The music of the restaurant was oddly loud in his ears.

"I didn't copy yours either. I suppose we both had the same good idea?"

"Yes! That's right," Lei said, relaxing.

"But who is Frank the Dragon? How did you get such a name?"

"I can send you a picture of him when I am home again," Lei said. "But where he came from is a much longer story."

Zheng An smiled at him. "Shall we order more food, then, do you think?"

Lei swallowed. "Maybe—after." He felt, sitting in the small restaurant with its gleaming surface and the buzz of other voices around him, like he was reaching for words. It felt like reaching for blocks of type to set in an old-style printing press. In his mind, his hand slid and patted over entire drawers of characters before alighting on the ones he needed to begin with.

"Almost three years ago, my best friend bought a cheap little dragon statue from a tourist vendor."

Zheng An's eyes widened a little and they leaned forward, just a hair, listening.

"He brought the little thing home and named it Frank and wouldn't hear a word against it."

"I can't wait to get your picture. Will you use photos of Frank in your encouragement texts from now on?"

"Yes, if you want me to. Logan would have liked that. But how are you?"

Zheng An could widen her eyes no further. Her lips had parted, just a touch, and Lei thought he found understanding in her face and a kind of supplication he did not quite expect. "You have helped me not to be fired from my job, Lei, and I am grateful. But there is something I need help to do and I do not think texts of encouragement will be enough."

"Oh?" Lei said, leaning forward without meaning to.

"I promised my sister I would go to our place, out in the country. It is not a temple—not to anyone but Connie. We used to go together. I am months late this year, because I cannot bear to go alone." Her breath caught a little. Lei knew he ought to avert his own gaze but could not.

"It is—unfair of me, asking you here and now," she said, covering her mouth with a hand.

"I will go with you right now if you wish me to," Lei said.

Relief came to An's face like a sunrise through rain. "Please."

They did not speak on the train that rushed away from their station twenty minutes later, only stared at the landscape streaming past.

"This one," An said, speaking for the first time since boarding.

Lei nodded and followed her onto a quiet platform. He could hear birds and moving water but no delivery bikes revving. The train was rapidly fading into the distance.

"Here." An took them down a narrow street whose pavement gave way to packed earth. A hill rose off to one side. Lei felt Frank in his pocket as he walked, following An down a fork in the path. The hill got closer and Lei thought he recognized the stone as granite. It seemed beautiful to him though the muscles of his legs were beginning to ache. He didn't often need to walk long distances, the city being so self-contained.

An did not seem to notice him tiring though sweat beaded her own forehead as she pushed on, only halting before a shallow pool fed by a waterfall that scattered sunlight. Here, she smiled, the furrows smoothing from her brow.

"Hello, Mei-Mei," she said. She reached into her pocket and took out a sweet package. She opened it and placed a mooncake on a stone near the water. "I still remember they're your favorite," she said, before turning to Lei and offering him another.

"Sorry I'm late," An said. "I won't take so long again."

The mooncake was a little stale but sweet on Lei's tongue as he listened to the waterfall stream into the pool and stroked Frank's head with a thumb.

Rachel Lippolis

The Year Alice Turned Ten

Alice was sure of three things. First, the Cincinnati Reds were definitely going to win the 2000 World Series. They had Ken Griffey, Jr., in outfield, Barry Larkin at shortstop, and Danny Graves in relief. No other team could beat them. The second thing Alice knew for sure was that only beige foods were edible. Bread and plain noodles were fine; grilled cheese and pepperoni pizza were not. And third, her mom Darla Gooding was never ever getting married. Her mom was pretty and all, she just didn't like being around other people or having regular conversations. The two of them would live alone forever, or until Alice turned eighteen and left for college or the Army, whichever wouldn't make her eat non-beige food.

Living only with her mom wasn't so bad. After school, Alice walked past identical apartment buildings and used the key hanging around her neck to let herself into their small unit. She ate crackers, watched cartoons or baseball with the volume so high the neighbors banged on the ceiling, and waited for her mom to get home. Three or four days a week, her mom did makeup and styling at Walker Funeral Home. Sometimes she brought home leftover flower arrangements that were taller than Alice, making all five rooms smell nauseatingly floral. She told Alice stories of reconstructing noses and contouring cheek bones.

"Is it scary?" Alice asked. She pictured a room full of dead bodies, their spirits dancing around the ceiling.

"I was nervous the first time, but I got used to it. And styling dead bodies pays better than doing makeup on live ones. Fewer complaints, too." Her mom laughed. She was always laughing at things Alice didn't think were funny.

Both had brown frizzy hair, large hazel eyes, and a preference for toffee ice cream. But, as far as Alice could tell, that was where their similarities ended. Alice was the shortest and skinniest girl in her fourth-grade class. At recess, she hid at the edge of the play yard, far enough from the action that she couldn't get hurt.

Her mom, on the other hand, was not fragile. "You're like one of those baseball players that can hit but isn't too fast, so they stick you out in right field," Alice said once. "You're tall and sturdy, like Dmitri Young."

"Who?"

"He's on the Reds."

"Gee, thanks," her mom replied. But Alice hadn't meant it as an insult. She was solid. Strong. Unlike her father, who'd left before Alice was even born.

Alice squirmed as her mom brushed her cheeks with blush. "That tickles!"

"Quit wiggling! If you move like that while I put on the mascara, I might poke an eye out."

But it was hard to hold still in the "preparation" room, the same place where bodies were embalmed and dressed. The room was cold and windowless and smelled like chemicals. Alice had forgotten to bring her housekey to school, so her mom picked her up and brought her back to her work, where Alice watched her apply special makeup to a pale, wrinkly corpse. By the time her mom had finished, the body resembled an older woman in the midst of a restful sleep.

Her mom applied eyeshadow over Alice's left eyelid. Alice pretended to be a statue. Frozen. Dead, like the old woman. "Is this the same stuff you use on dead people?"

"Didn't you notice you're wearing the same shade as Mrs. Thompson over there? Stop moving!"

Her mom used her finger to smudge the area over Alice's eye and then repeated the process on her right eye.

"I talked to your father yesterday. He's moving back to Cincinnati. He has a job and apartment lined up. He's excited to spend time with you."

Alice had never met her father, Mike. She wanted to jump out of her chair and ask a million questions but instead told herself to be a statue. Be dead.

Her mom slowly lined the bottom of Alice's eyes with a special pencil. "We'll take it slow, I promise. I didn't ask for him to come back . . . You just say the word, and I'll make him leave and never return. Oh, Ali, don't cry. You'll ruin the makeup."

"Well, look at you," Mike said the first time he visited their apartment. "You're practically a teenager."

Alice recognized her father's voice, low and exaggerated, from when he called on her birthday last August. And she knew his face, from the high school yearbook her mom had saved, his eyes half-closed as if struggling to stay open.

But he was different than Alice expected.

A bumpy pink-red scar covered the left side of his face, from below his eye to his chin. It started out narrow over his cheek then widened as it went down. The scar hadn't been in the yearbook photo, and her mom hadn't mentioned it. Alice held out her hand to touch the scar, but he stepped back.

"I'm sorry," she said. Besides the scar, Alice thought he was the one who looked like a teenager, not her. Skinny and awkward, wearing a baggy, long-sleeved shirt and jeans that were frayed at the bottom, he stared at Alice without blinking. He was four or five inches shorter than her mom.

"It looks a lot better," her mom finally said.

"Where'd it come from?" Alice asked.

"You never told her?" he said in a near-whisper. "Alice, I'll let your mom fill you in. Here." He gave her a San Diego Padres ballcap, from the last place he lived, then stepped backward toward the door. "I've got to catch my bus."

"Stay for dinner?"

"Another time." Mike turned around and walked out without another word.

The entire visit lasted five minutes; no one even sat down. Her mom stood at the edge of the kitchen. The smile she'd worn when he first walked in had disappeared.

Alice begged her mom to tell her about the scar. Where did it come from? Why hadn't he visited before? But she might as well have been talking to a corpse.

To start, he came on Wednesdays. The three of them sat around the kitchen table eating whatever her mom picked up on the way home from work. That first Wednesday, Alice tore apart her chicken nuggets as her mom asked about her geometry quiz, and her dad looked back and forth between the two of them while sipping Coke through a straw.

After dinner, Alice put on the Reds game. "Harris had a 3.75 ERA last year."

Her dad sat on the couch, an empty cushion between them. "Oh yeah?"

She explained that the Reds starting pitcher had earned $275,000 last year and was due to make over $1 million this season. "He better do well," Alice said.

"Pedro Martinez made $11 million last year," her dad said. "He throws the ball every five games and makes more money than we'll see in a lifetime."

Milwaukee was batting first. Alice glanced at her mom, still in the kitchen preparing a beige snack of saltines and peanut butter. Her mom nodded as if to say, *It's okay. You can sit near your father.*

She fell asleep on the couch by the seventh inning—the Reds were down big—and her dad was already gone when her mom gently nudged her awake. "Let's go to bed, Ali."

Those Wednesday evenings became a ritual. After dinner, Alice and her dad watched baseball while her mom read in the kitchen. They tried to get her to join them, but she always told them her book was far more interesting than watching grown men try to hit balls.

Alice made sure she sat on his left side. She waited until he seemed totally focused on the game, telling the pitcher he should throw a fastball, or yelling at the guy on first to stay close to the bag. When she was sure he wouldn't notice, Alice stared at his scar. She imagined how he got it and what it felt like, but mostly she thought about its shape. One night it was an upside-down tornado. Another, it was a tiny person standing on a hill. Alice wanted to ask her dad about it, but she liked having him around, and she didn't want to scare him off.

The door to their apartment was unlocked when Alice arrived home from school, Thursday afternoon. She hung her key back around her neck and stood just inside. The living room and kitchen were empty.

"Mom?" she called softly, peeking first in her own bedroom and then the bathroom. Then she knocked on her mom's door while slowly pushing it open.

She caught a glimpse of her parents, in bed, clothes strewn about the room, before her mom yelled, "Close the door!"

Alice ran to her own room, slammed the door, and climbed onto the bed and buried herself under the covers. She pulled all the sheets over her head then closed her eyes to add one more barrier. Outside were muffled voices and then footsteps.

"Sorry about that, Ali," her mom said. "He's gone. Are you okay?"

Alice pretended to be asleep and didn't answer. Her mom yanked the covers from the bed and told Alice they were going for a walk.

The two walked in silence until they reached a small park Alice visited as a child. "You want to talk about what you saw? You must be mortified."

Alice shook her head.

"Your father and I were young when I got pregnant with you. We were practically kids, ourselves."

Alice said she knew that, and sat on one of the swings. Her mom sat on the swing next to her.

"Is he going to move in with us? Do you love him?"

"I don't know. How would you feel about that?"

Alice shrugged then pushed back and forth on the chains of the swing, going faster and higher; she waited until the swing was fully extended forward and jumped.

"Ali!"

Her feet hit the ground first. She tumbled forward, scraping her knees, shins, and elbows.

"Are you okay?" her mom yelled, rushing to her side.

Everything ached, but Alice was fine. "Tell me how Dad got his scar."

"You're relentless, Ali. It was a car accident. I was driving. We'd both been drinking."

"But you don't drink."

"No, not now. Back then, we were *always* drinking. I only had a few scrapes, but your dad was in worse shape. That was when I found out I was pregnant. I stopped drinking; he wouldn't. So I told him he couldn't be in your life, not until he decided to get sober."

"He's sober now?"

"Yeah." The two of them got on their swings again and started going back and forth, much more slowly.

Once school let out for the summer, Alice saw a lot more of her dad. He came over on weekdays when he wasn't needed at the warehouse, and they'd stay in the apartment watching *The Price is Right* and *Days of Our Lives*. After he got a used car, a Buick sedan, they drove all around the city, sometimes going to the zoo or children's museum. He didn't talk much, but Alice didn't mind. In a dark room at the aquarium, they stood in front of a tank full of small, tentacled jellyfish that glowed pink and blue. "Those are so cool," Alice said.

"It's bioluminescence," he said, stretching the word out into six distinct syllables.

Alice looked up at him, his face a silhouette but the white of his eyes glowing. "You and Mom should get married."

Alice never caught her parents together again, not like that, but she found other clues her mom might be happy. Her mom stopped frowning and crossing her arms when he complained about his job at the warehouse. Instead, she put her hand on his arm and nodded her head, saying things like, "Mmm-hmm" and "That must be hard."

His voice softened at her touch. "Actually, it's not that bad, Darla."

By August, it was clear the Reds weren't going to win the World Series. But when her dad showed her the three tickets he'd bought to celebrate her tenth birthday, Alice shrieked and threw her arms around him.

"Right behind third base. You can shout at Aaron Boone and he might wave to you," her dad said.

The afternoon before the game, her dad washed and cut half a dozen strawberries for Alice. "Something red for my Reds fan," he said, laughing.

She stared at the bowl of fruit and then at her mom, who raised her eyebrows and shrugged. Her mom still didn't say anything when

Alice, hands shaking and heart pounding, put a piece in her mouth. Alice closed her eyes as she chewed and chewed, grimacing as the reddish pink stuff filled the space between her teeth.

Alice opened her eyes, the sweet, broken-down strawberry now between her teeth and cheek, and spit the food on the floor. "I'm sorry. I'm so sorry!"

Her dad's eyes narrowed. "What was wrong with it?"

"It was red," Darla said.

The scar on his face became an erupting volcano. "You've got to be kidding me. It's not like I asked her to eat dog shit. Aren't you going to say something to your daughter?"

"*Our* daughter." Her mom grabbed a wet rag and began cleaning the floor. It wasn't much, maybe half a strawberry. Alice knelt down next to her mom and said she didn't mean to do it.

"I know," her mom said quietly.

"We're still going tomorrow, right?"

Alice's dad was late picking them up for the game. Alice paced around the living room in her Griffey jersey and San Diego Padres cap, certain that she'd ruined everything by spitting out that strawberry. She'd never heard him talk like that before. She said those words to herself, *Dog Shit*, over and over, until they stopped making her stomach sink.

But when he finally showed up, it was like nothing had happened. "Happy early birthday, kiddo. You won't believe these seats," he said, grinning like one of the boys in her class. He had on a plain red T-shirt, jeans, and a baseball cap.

Soon after they were seated—Alice between her parents—a dozen men unrolled a giant tarp to cover the infield, anticipating a rain delay.

"This is ridiculous." Her dad shifted back and forth in the plastic red seat. "There's not a drop of rain in that sky."

"Maybe they know something we don't," her mom said. Within moments, rain began to pummel the tarp; everyone around them jumped from their seats and hurried up the concrete stairs for shelter. Her mom stood. "Let's go, Ali—"

"No!" Her dad banged his fist on the empty seat in front of him. "I mean, this is fun, right? I'm sure it'll pass. Don't go."

"Let's stay, Mom. It's just rain."

Alice's actual birthday wasn't for another three days, but this was the first one that felt special. She knew her dad was upset, but Alice was practically giddy about the delay making the game even longer. She looked back and forth between her parents and hoped this was just the beginning. Soon, maybe the three of them would go to the zoo or for walks along the river.

The rain fell in big, heavy drops for about five minutes and then slowed to a drizzle. When her dad left for refreshments, someone tossed a beach ball in right field; the colorful ball was batted around the stadium before landing on the stadium steps and rolling between some empty seats. Her mom hunched over a novel, letting her back protect the paper from the rain. Her dad brought her nachos, with cheese on the side. He also had a half-empty cup of beer that he stuck under his seat and held a finger to his lips: "Shh!"

When the game finally began, the crowd was smaller and quieter. She shouted "Boone!" when Aaron Boone caught a pop foul not twenty feet from their seats, and she jumped to her feet when the small crowd attempted the wave.

"Okay, okay," her dad said after the St. Louis Cardinals finished batting in the fourth. He reached over Alice and grabbed the book from her mom. "Both of you, look at the jumbotron."

In dotted letters, Alice read, "Happy 30th birthday, Rob!" followed by, "Happy 52nd birthday, Chris!" Alice's heart felt like it was going to jump out of her chest, and she was scared she'd blink and miss her name. "Happy 25th anniversary, Tim and Sue!"

"Come on," her dad muttered.

"Welcome Boy Scout troop 161!"

Alice glanced at her dad then back to the screen that read, "Darla, will you marry me?"

Her pang of disappointment turned to excitement. She saw the three of them living in a small house with a backyard and fence. She'd change her last name to her dad's, Morelli. Goodbye, Alice Gooding! But her mom's expression seemed to go from confused to horrified as Alice's dad pulled a ring out of his jean pocket and stood on an empty seat in the row in front of them. "What do you say?"

Alice wanted to shake her dad or pull him up into a hug. Wasn't it obvious?

"No, Mike. I say no."

He opened his mouth as if to say something. Instead, he handed the ring, a plain gold band, to Alice, and shoved his way to the stadium steps. Alice started to run after him, but her mom held her back.

"Why would you say no?"

When her mom didn't answer, Alice shook free and sprinted up the stairs. Away from the field and assigned seats, the stadium was chaotic. Globs of people moved in all directions—toward the stands, out of the bathrooms, into never-ending lines. Alice nearly ran into a man staring at a television showing the exact same game that was on the field. She opened her hand; the ring was still there.

A burst of cheers and applause flooded the stadium. Alice looked up at the television to see a replay of Ken Griffey, Jr., her favorite player, hitting a line-drive home run into center field. The staring man turned to Alice, said, "Yes!" and held out his hand for a high five.

Alice whooped, tapped her shirt with one hand, then slapped his hand with the other. She turned in a circle, and all the people around her were smiling or slapping hands. It was like everyone in the stadium had been holding their breaths and were finally exhaling.

The ring! Alice held out her hands—both empty. She crouched down on the hard, dirty floor and saw only smooshed pieces of popcorn and straw wrappers around her. "No no no no no!"

Then she heard him.

"Five dollars for a cup of piss beer? Come on!"

By the sound of her dad's voice, he'd already had another beer or two. Alice pulled her knees close to her chest, her back against a sticky garbage can, and closed her eyes.

Then she felt the familiar touch of her mom's hands. "Let's go, Ali."

"I dropped the ring. Help me find it!"

Her mom said it was fine. The ring didn't matter. "I've got your dad's keys. He can take the bus."

Alice didn't cry until they reached the car. But once she started, she could barely catch her breath between sobs. Her mom looked straight ahead as she pulled onto the road, wearing the same expression she had when spackling makeup on a dead woman. Alice wiped her face with her shirt and pulled the bill of her ballcap down to hide her eyes.

Alice was alone when her dad came by the apartment the next day for his keys. They sat together on the couch, staring at the blank television set. Maybe he was waiting for her to talk first, but she didn't know what to say.

His scar was just an upside-down triangle. It wasn't bright with sweat, like it had been at the baseball game or after she spit out the strawberry. He no longer flinched when Alice looked at it, no matter how deeply she stared. She reached out her index finger and held it an inch from the scar. He didn't say anything or move away, so she lay her finger on the triangle's apex and traced each bumpy edge down to the base. The scar was smoother than she expected. "It really doesn't hurt?"

"Not one bit." He gently removed her hand from his face. "Let's go for a drive, kiddo. Get some ice cream."

Alice was thinking about all the beige flavors to choose from— mocha, peanut butter, toffee, even vanilla seemed close enough—as they reached his car. Her dad tried to unlock the passenger door for her, but the key didn't fit. He tried another, and it wouldn't move either. When the next one didn't work, he dropped the set of keys on the sidewalk, muttering "Goddamnit."

He's drunk, she thought. When he finally got the key to work, she stood there, frozen. "Let's go," he said. "What's the problem?"

Her Padres cap sat on the passenger seat. She thought about how disappointed he must have been. Heartbroken, even. She hopped inside the car, put the cap on her head, and buckled her seatbelt. Alice inhaled, checking for that spoiled apple scent from his breath she'd noticed lately. She only smelled peppermint. "There's no problem."

He pulled onto the street, another car honking at him. "Roll down your window, the air condition's out."

The traffic light turned red, but her dad wasn't slowing. "Dad!" she yelled as everything went black.

"I'm definitely traumatizing you," her mom said. With Alice and her mother on either side, her father's body lay on the table at Walker Funeral Home. A colder, paler version of the live one. He'd died almost instantly, not that Alice remembered anything from the accident.

"The first thing I'm using is a topical scar makeup. It will make the left side of his face as smooth as his right side." Her mom pulled out a thick, beige cream for his cheek and a wedge-shaped sponge. "Now I'm going to apply concealer. This is just like what you'd get at a drug store."

"Can I do it?" Alice asked.

Without a word, her mom handed her a makeup brush and compact. Alice climbed onto a stool so that the table was level with her waist. His eyes were shut, and his lips close together. "Dog shit," Alice said, when a tear started to well up. "Dog shit dog shit dog shit," she repeated until the moment was over, and she was steady again. Then, she carefully applied the concealer to each cheek. Without the scar, he was a sleeping version of his yearbook picture.

Alice stepped down, and her mom pulled her into a hug. "Ouch," Alice said, still sore from the accident. "Can I be alone with him?"

He'd been her father for ten years, but he only acted like one for five months. Nothing would really change with him gone. The Reds were underperforming. Non-beige food was still gross. And her mom was still alone.

Alice would always believe it was her fault he had died. If she hadn't encouraged him, or if she had tried to convince her mom to say yes, or if she hadn't gotten in the car, or if she hadn't been born . . . There were so many ways for her father to still be alive, and only one for him to be dead.

"I'm so sorry, Dad."

Her mom would be back soon, so she had to act quickly. Using a cotton ball and makeup remover, Alice scrubbed his left cheek—first gently, then more vigorously—until the triangle again revealed itself. The scar was an upside-down heart.

Jennifer Schomburg Kanke

The Sparing of the Snails

The girl next door was throwing snails over the back fence again, yelling "yeet" as she launched each one into the air. Oscar's inclination was to let it slide. This was not a big enough infraction to warrant talking to her mother. Greta felt differently, so Oscar was soon running a comb through his thinning hair and looking for his clean pants.

"What if Badger finds them and eats one? Go over and ask her to cut it out, just go."

The chances of their monstrous chocolate Lab getting lungworm from the neighbors' snails was low, and it was all very treatable if caught early, so he wasn't quite sure what the hubbub was about. But his marriage to Greta had worked so well for the last thirty years because he did whatever Greta said, and Greta only said what she thought he might be likely to do anyway.

The dog had come to them after their son Kyle's divorce, delivered in his crate by their newly ex-daughter-in-law who had gotten him in the settlement just to spite Kyle but had not actually wanted the dog herself. Oscar thought she was letting Kyle off easy. If he'd cheated on Greta with a waitress from that dive *Rodrigo's*, Greta would have taken more than just his dog.

He knew precious little about the woman next door, only that she was single and in her mid-thirties. He knew she had a daughter who was around eight, maybe nine. Old enough to know you shouldn't fling stuff into the neighbors' yard, but young enough not to care. Oscar thought that must be a beautiful sweet spot to be in.

He was old enough to care about every consequence, and had been for quite a while. His mind was an endless list of consequences at all times. It really was the secret to his success, he felt. How much trouble had he avoided by worrying his way around it? All these kids nowadays talking about anxiety and self-care drove Oscar a little nuts. Anxiety keeps you on the straight and narrow, anxiety helps you keep your mid-level management job at Panhandle

Savings and Loan even when the consultant from corporate comes through looking for ways to rightsize the budget. Twenty years he'd been there, fifteen as Assistant Director for Small Business Loans. You didn't get that far on bubble baths and yoga nidras, he could tell you that much.

Four years ago, when they'd turned fifty, Greta had gotten into all that stuff. Lavender bath bombs on Sunday nights. Listening to "Healing Darkness for Sleep" on her phone before bed. Working out to those Pahla B videos for "women of a certain age." The YouTuber's positivity bothered Oscar, a lot. "Just remember, whatever you're doing, it's enough" and "not every day needs to be a push day." What a load of crap! Whether or not he was enough had never crossed Oscar's mind. If he stopped to think about it, though he saw no reason to, he knew he wasn't enough and never would be. This was fine (again, if he stopped to think about it, which he saw no reason to do), as it kept Oscar on his toes since he was not a man of good birth or infinite charisma. He had only his own hard work to fall back on. He was an assistant director at one of the largest banks serving North Florida and southern Georgia, and that felt about right to him.

"What am I supposed to say to her when I get over there?" he asked his wife as he headed out the front door.

"Just tell her to stop her kid from throwing the snails in our yard. It's really not that hard, Oscar." She moved toward the kitchen to start some vegetables steaming for dinner. Oscar was grateful for the built-in excuse the meal provided. No matter how the confrontation went, it couldn't go on for long. The food was nearly ready, so he just had to get back home, you see. Just had to.

All the houses in the neighborhood looked much alike with their slight variations on the brick ranch. Double windows in the living room and two bedrooms along the front, the primary bedroom with an en suite in the back. It was comforting to know that in every house on Portland Avenue the rooms were all exactly where they should be. The yards, on the other hand, were where everyone's personalities really came through, to Oscar's chagrin.

Greta and Oscar had gone classic North Florida with their yard. Two sago palms by the walk, hot pink azaleas to hide the house's concrete slab foundation, and monkey grass encircling the water oaks that Oscar swore were live oaks. Sometimes Greta would put a petunia or two in a pot on the porch, but not much more than that. It wasn't too stately, just the way Oscar liked it.

The neighbor woman kept her yard a bit differently. Pentas, salvia, passion vine, plumbago, and milkweed. The front yard had very little grass, and only a small meandering path of mulch led the way through the riot of color with no rhyme or reason. Had they lived in a better neighborhood, Oscar would have considered bringing her yard up to the HOA, but as it was they didn't have one, so he just complained to Greta about how trashy it made everything look.

As he approached the house he tried desperately to remember the woman's name. Addressing her by name would allow him to appear friendly, the picture of the good neighbor, while also giving him the upper hand. He knew her name not because they had ever actually met but because the mail carrier sometimes accidentally delivered her Title IX and Athleta catalogs to Oscar and Greta by mistake. Greta would thumb through them while sitting on the toilet and briefly contemplate buying one of their fancy sports bras or yoga pants before pitching them in the recycling. What was her name again? Stacy? Tracy? Macy? No, not Macy. Casey, her name was Casey. He was all set to continue his march to her front door and say, "Now listen here, Casey. That child of yours is out of control. If our Badger gets lungworm from those snails, you'll be paying the vet bill, you will."

But as he stepped up to the porch he noticed that sitting in a chair, partially hidden behind a wall of shampoo ginger and red canna lilies, was the child in question herself. She was not at that moment crying, but it was clear to Oscar that she had quite recently been doing so. What was also becoming clear to Oscar was that she was not nearly as young as he'd originally thought she was. At one time he had been very good at guessing the ages of children. When Kyle was still in school he'd get it right eight out of ten times, missing only the late bloomers and early maturers. Now he had to resort to general groupings: baby, toddler, kid, tween, teen. He'd put the girl in the right group but had her on the wrong end of it. She was closer to twelve than eight, her face losing its baby fat roundness, her shoulders hunching forward to hide her breasts. When he realized he'd been mistaken about her age, he felt a small center of heat buried somewhere deep beneath the swirling consequences and details in his mind. He'd felt this kind of thing before and knew that it would only grow hotter and hotter, like a burner on an electric range that starts out cold and warms and warms and warms until it's glowing red and singeing the untidied remains of last night's dinner off its edges. This girl had activated the electric range of his heart. At eight it was okay to not care about how your actions affected others, but by twelve—TWELVE—you really should be getting your act together. Clearly this snailthrower of a girl was not growing into a good person. She was building a small and mean heart deep down inside and something must eventually be done about it by someone.

"Are you okay?" He finally decided to ask, quite intentionally not asking what was wrong, because that *someone* who would eventually do *something* about her was most assuredly not going to be him, if he had any say in the matter.

"No, I lost my bracelet. The one Granny gave me right before we moved down here." She said this as if Oscar was intimately acquainted with her and her grandmother enough to care about this bracelet.

"When did you have it last?" He didn't care, but if he could help, why not help, right?

"I had it on when I was yeeting the . . ." She looked away from him and became overly fascinated with her shoes. There was a time when Oscar would have been able to tell if the black and white emblem on their side was a knockoff or the real deal, would have recognized the logo on her lightweight hoodie enough to tell if she was one of the cool kids or not. Kyle had always been one of the cool kids. Oscar had not been and took Kyle's successes as a testament to his parenting skills rather than genetics.

"Ah, I see."

"Sorry?"

The electric range of his heart grew hotter and hotter the longer he talked to her. Was she sorry or not, for Pete's sake? Oscar looked in her eyes to see if there was remorse, to see if the corners crinkled or her brow furrowed. Give a guy something to work with, kid! He saw no sign of any emotion in her face, just a patiently blank stare. She sounded so much like the new cashier at work whenever he asked her if she'd seen some television show or other, like she was ready to change course if it turned out to be the wrong answer. "Brit, do you watch *Midsomer Murders*?" "No?"

Kids these days! This neighbor girl had no respect for anything, none of them did. She really just needed some structure, which she clearly wasn't getting here if she was hurling stuff over fences. Oscar prepared a lecture in his mind like the kind that had always been effective with Kyle.

"Listen, you have to respect property lines, it's the only way neighborhood living works. Your yard, my yard. Your stuff, my stuff." Kyle had always wanted to know why things were, and Oscar had spent untold breaths two decades ago trying to convince his boy that it wasn't the why that mattered but the what. "Here's what happens in the world; adjust yourself accordingly," was the stinger he put to the end of each lecture. It was the way Kyle would know the conversation was done and he was free to go.

Oscar was about to launch into his lecture for real when the girl spoke again.

"You're not going to tell my mom, are you? About the snails?" She seemed younger again, smaller.

"That was my intention, yes."

"Please don't. I just didn't know what else to do with them."

"One option would have been to leave them in your own garden, I would think."

The girl, whose name he learned was Nora, explained that her mother had offered her ten dollars a week to keep the snails off the petunias and zinnias. Her mother's suggestion was to put out small saucers of beer so they would drown, or she could pick them off the leaves and crush them with a rock. Whichever way Nora wanted was fine. Casey trusted her choices and told her so, which was why, Nora explained to a patiently waiting Oscar, she absolutely-for-totally-sure must not be told that Nora had decided to yeet them over the fence into Oscar and Greta's yard instead.

"Why didn't you just do what your mother asked?" Oscar felt like he was meeting with the guy from the Gadsden Street Grub and Suds all over again. He'd spent days helping the young man come up with a viable business plan, only to watch him chuck the whole thing and invest the loan money in scratch-and-sniff menus instead of needed maintenance on the business's oldest industrial-size washers or fixing the element on the deep fryer. He'd never understand these people who just did whatever. Why couldn't they stop and think things through like a normal person?

Nora looked aghast. "You think I'd want to kill someone? I'm not a monster."

"They're not someone, they're snails. That's how gardening works. The bugs kill the plants so the gardeners kill the bugs." He could feel himself getting on a roll. Maybe he'd make that speech after all.

"Snails aren't bugs, they're terrestrial gastropod mollusks." She was matter-of-fact and not really as repentant as Oscar felt someone in her position should be.

"You're missing the point." Oscar tried to explain again to the girl how gardening works, about her rights and responsibilities in this particular situation.

"No, *you're* missing the point." She was practically yelling now and had stood up from her chair to add gravitas to her words, "I'm . . . not . . . killing . . . any . . . one. End of story."

Nora was more stubborn than Kyle had been at her age, and Oscar searched the anxiety files in his head trying to figure out the right tack to take to get her to understand why what she'd done was so wrong.

Then he realized something very important about the girl. She was not his child. He did not need to make her understand. He did not need to make her a better person; that was on her parents. All he needed to do was stop her from throwing snails in his yard. He'd gotten hung up on the "why" of it all and lost track of the "what," like he was Kyle or something.

"Okay, okay. Could you just, could you just 'yeet' the other way toward Mrs. Bryant's next time?"

"Sure. Pleasure doing business with you." She stuck her hand out like he'd just helped her sign a lease on some hot College Town bar or fitness studio. She was confident she'd negotiated the deal of a lifetime. They shook on it and he headed back home through the wildflowers.

"Well?" Greta asked when he came through the door.

"Taken care of, my dear. All taken care of." He kissed her cheek and gave her arm a squeeze.

"Good. Thank you. Was that so hard?"

Later, after he'd finished his steamed broccoli and quinoa, he sat in the backyard playing ball with Badger. If he could tire the dog out sufficiently, there was an eighty percent chance he wouldn't force open the door to the linen closet at two a.m. and eat a bar of soap tonight, as he had last night, or move four rolls of toilet paper from the closet to the living room floor, as he had the night before that. They had played back and forth a few minutes when Badger came back, not with the slobber-covered tennis ball Oscar expected, but something else entirely.

"What you got there, boy?" He took a small string of beads from the dog's mouth. They were a cheap and green plastic like the kind Greta sometimes picked up from the display near the register at Talbots as an afterthought, just something little to pull this or that outfit together. But he didn't recognize it as any of hers and realized it must be the one the girl had lost earlier in the day. Oscar considered marching back over and giving it to Casey, forcing Nora to explain to her mother how it had ended up on Oscar's side of the fence. Really, though, he'd had enough excitement for the day. Plus, they'd shook on it. Instead, he pulled his arm back over his head, and with significant vim and vigor sent the bracelet sailing back over the fence, hollering "yeet."

Donna Wojnar Dzurilla

Winning at 1972

Peg preferred that Buck work daylight, but he preferred night shift, especially in the summer. He'd lose the quarter-an-hour shift differential and be stuck working in the heat if he switched to day turn. The mill created its own sense of chaos, heightened by the noise, the smell of molten metal, and the ever-present potential for accidents, but at night the sky contained it.

The 160-inch rolling mill's locker room held the summer heat even at 7:00 a.m. The sound of steel-toed work boots tapping the bottom rail of the stainless-steel sink interrupted the sympatico and rhythm of conversations. To operate the sink and wash up, the men tapped the metal rail that circled the bottom of the birdbath-shaped pedestal like the gas pedal of a car. The giant circular sink, with spigots on top in the center, and large enough in diameter to accommodate eight men washing their hands at one time, filled the space between the toilets in the locker room and the entrance from the shop floor. Nightshift workers washed up, then jockeyed for space with the incoming daylight crew to sit along the benches that ran between the lockers. Some showered, but most only wanted to change out of their work clothes as quick as they could, to either head home or meet up at a bar for a cold bottle of Iron City.

Buck changed out of his work boots into his everyday garden stompers, but stopped when he noticed the bottoms of his steel-toed boots. The leather upper was starting to pull away from the sole of the right boot, but he figured he'd get another month out of them. He'd get a voucher for a new pair of boots at the next safety meeting.

Someone came up behind Buck and elbowed him in the back. He lost his balance and almost fell off the bench. Buck turned and stood, ready to take a swing at whoever knocked into him. During shift changes, the mill locker room reminded him of high school.

"Watch where you're going, you son-of-a-" Buck stopped before finishing his curse when he saw it was his buddy, Angelo.

Buck dropped the boot he held onto the bench and offered his hand. At six foot tall, he towered over his friend. "What are you doing in here? It's a hell of a walk from, what, O.H. #5? Isn't that where you're laying brick this week?"

"What were you gonna do, take a swing at me? I don't care how tall you are. You'd lose that one, my friend," Angelo said. "Squirty's covering for me. He owes me. You know Squirty. He has the kid in the wheelchair. I have something I got to talk to you about. Couldn't wait."

Angelo, at five-foot-five, was shorter than most workers, but formidable. His neck, arms and shoulders were thick and sinewy, and like Buck's were well-developed by the years they worked alongside each other shoveling slag on the labor gang at the U. S. Steel Duquesne Works. Angelo's close-cropped hair remained thick and showed no sign of balding. Black, shiny ringlets reacted to the heat and clung to his scalp. His brown eyes were almost black, and his cheeks had a ruddiness that his olive-toned skin couldn't hide. He was a handsome man, and he knew it. Work on the masonry gang kept Angelo in shape.

Angelo had lost his wife young. Buck and Peg stood for him and Lydia on their wedding day. They had two years as husband and wife until she died during the premature birth of their only child. His son didn't survive the delivery. Underdeveloped lungs, the doctors said. Angelo never remarried. Peg occasionally brought up the subject of Angelo remarrying to Buck, and was met with silence. Buck knew better than to suggest it. No one could take Lydia's place. Angelo had gone through a dark time and Buck refused to remind him of it.

"You catch the second half of that double header yesterday?" Buck asked as he sat down on the bench and shifted over to make room for Angelo.

"Sure did. Did you see Pops hit that second homer?"

"Heard that and heard him bat five other guys in."

"You still just listening to games on the radio? I'm telling you, watch it on television and bring yourself into the twentieth century."

"Nah, television shows me what they want me to see. Bob Prince on the radio lets me imagine the whole field," Buck said as he grabbed a garden stomper. He noticed, before pulling it on, his big toe had poked a hole through his socks. He'd have Peg pick him up a pack of work socks.

"Want to go in on a number with me?" Angelo asked. "My Uncle Vince—you know him, they got him working the #4 blowing engine house—collects for the fifty-fifty. He has one number left. I told him to hold it for me."

"How much? How much payoff?"

"Twenty a pop. Fifty-fifty payout with half going back to Vince and the family," Angelo replied. "They top the intake. If we split the buy-in of twenty bucks and hit, at ten grand, that's five a piece."

Buck worked his wallet out of his back pocket. He pulled out a ten and handed it to Angelo. "When are you getting the ticket?"

"Uncle Vince is on daylight. I'll catch him during shift change tomorrow or drop by his place. Feel like stopping for a beer?" Angelo asked.

"Nah, I'm heading straight home. Peg needs the car."

Buck slapped Angelo on the back.

"How's my goddaughter? She'll be wanting behind the wheel soon. Sweet sixteen isn't far off."

"Don't remind me. Her and Peg, well, I hope Louise makes it to sixteen without Peg ringing her neck," said Buck.

"I remember how my sisters were. Give them a couple years and they'll be best friends."

They walked together until they reached the gate and separated to find their cars.

Buck thought about Peg's hairdresser appointment at 8:30 (sharp, she'd reminded him) and the grief he'd get if he was late getting home with the car. He slid behind the wheel and joined the line of cars heading out towards Eighth Avenue.

The rest of the week passed slowly. Sirens signaling an accident rang out towards the end of his shift on Friday morning. They'd gone ninety days without one. It wasn't a record, but it was a long stretch of no one getting hurt. Buck made a quick sign of the cross.

Word made its way around that somebody broke a couple fingers on the 48-inch rolling mill. Once he heard it was just some busted fingers, he knew nobody had died. Once an iron slab loaded everyone was careful, but while leading up to it people got sloppy. It would have happened when the upper and lower rollers engaged just prior to slab load. Most likely some guy didn't pull his hand out quick enough.

Busted fingers would heal, and the guy could still work. No one he knew had reason to be at the 48-inch. Accidents occurred. Nobody died. It was part of the job.

He looked forward to meeting up with Angelo after next turn and seeing if their number hit. Buck and Angelo met in 1953 when they started out on the labor gang at U.S. Steel's Duquesne Works. After Buck graduated from high school, his dad insisted he leave Uniontown and move to the city because he didn't want him in the Keystone mines or working Frick's beehive coke ovens in the nearby coal town of Shoaf. Buck couldn't wait to leave the patch behind and see the city. Pittsburgh was only an hour away from Uniontown, but it felt like he was getting out and seeing the world. Towns with thriving business districts, like Homestead, Duquesne, and McKeesport surrounded the mills in the valley. Angelo's Uncle Vince worked at Homestead, along with Angelo's other uncles and cousins. Angelo graduated from Central Catholic and his Uncle Vince pulled some strings to get him in at Duquesne Works.

In 1952, President Truman nationalized the steel industry to avoid a worker walkout and strike. The steel companies sued, the U. S. Supreme Court ruled, and the president lost. The president's attempt to avert a wildcat strike failed and, in less than two months, the steel companies settled and ironically agreed to the wage increase that the union had initially pushed for. In 1954, Duquesne Works hired and ran three shifts. It was a good time to work there. Production was up due to the Korean War. Buck and Angelo benefited from the negotiated wage increase without a strike or the loss of a paycheck. The men put in the mandatory ninety-day probationary period, after which they got their union cards. They put their years in and built up seniority to bid out of the labor pool into a unit. It took time for spots to open up to bid on. In 1964, Buck and Angelo built up enough seniority to bid out of Duquesne and into jobs at the Homestead Works.

In the 1950s nepotism and ethnicity determined the jobs a worker could bid. It was understood that was the way the mills ran. To bid out of Duquesne and into Homestead, Angelo bid into the all-Italian masonry gang and stayed there. Buck, like most men of eastern European descent, started as a scarfer. Scraping the crust off of molten iron as it flowed from a tapped furnace was a young man's job.

After Buck scarfed for a couple years, Peg tired of his burned clothes and body. Peg became friends at Christian Mothers with Joanne, the night foreman's wife. Ten months later, Buck successfully bid out of the furnace crew and into an inspector's job at the 160-inch mill. He grew used to being asked, "How the hell did you get an inspector's job with that Slovakian last name?" He'd just shrug and say, "Didn't you know Varga is an English, no, maybe a Scottish name?" That usually left the person asking the question speechless.

Buck and Angelo, like most of their fellow workers, thought of themselves as Homestead lifers. Their jobs were secure.

Buck punched out on Saturday morning at 7:00 a.m. in a jovial mood because it meant the end of another workweek. He looked forward to checking the paper to see what the number was. He slid his timecard back in his slot and moved forward with the line of men already punched out.

"Anybody have a paper?" Buck yelled out as he made his way to the locker room to change out of his work greens. Somebody always had a morning *Post-Gazette*. No one replied or no one wanted to share if they had one. Guys were funny that way. "Anybody?"

"Let it go," Angelo yelled over the din of conversations, sounds of lockers banging and noise from the shop floor.

Angelo walked over and met Buck at his locker. Guys coming on and off shift jostled them as they tried to have a conversation.

"I have to make a stop at the safety office. We can grab some breakfast at Straka's and either celebrate or cry in our beer. We'll pick up a paper on the way or find one someone left behind there."

Buck grabbed the navy windbreaker out of his locker. He didn't go anywhere without a coat. No matter what the weather, he wore a coat to cover his clothes. "Okay, Ang, I'll meet you there."

Angelo signaled to show Buck that he had heard him and left.

Buck gathered his things from his locker, then headed towards the main gate. As he approached the Amity Street mill gate, he let himself be drawn into one of the currents in the river of workers exiting the mill. He started off in the direction of his car, but changed his mind. It made no sense to move the car. There'd be no spots on Eighth Avenue during the shift change and once he crossed the railroad tracks in front of the main gate, it was a short walk to Straka's.

Buck picked up his pace. The morning sun promised another miserably hot day, and the air might hang heavy and smell, but he was outside the mill walls and beyond the gate. The shift was uneventful and the need for sleep hadn't hit him yet. He felt happy and hopeful. The odds were against it, but maybe, just maybe, they'd hit the number, and he could finally buy Peg a car.

Straka's Tavern was a short walk down Eighth Avenue. Buck threw a dime into the slot at the top of the metal *Pittsburgh Post-Gazette* newspaper box outside the tavern. He pulled at the door handle then wiggled the display copy from the metal grid that held the last copy in the window of the box's door. His eyes went to the corner above the masthead where the stock market closing numbers were listed.

2-8-9.

Holy shit!

He read it again.

They hit! Five thousand each. No more rushing home to get the car to Peg or listening to the guys ribbing him when Peg and the kids dropped him off or picked him up at the mill gate. He'd have his '70 Ford sedan to himself.

"Well, what's the word?"

Buck looked up to see Angelo lumber up the sidewalk. Angelo seemed winded from the walk. Seniority on the masonry gang meant more set-up and less hauling. The work wasn't as physically demanding as it was when he first bid it. Now Angelo's back hurt from bending, not from hauling a brick hod over his shoulder.

Buck knew without needing to hear what Angelo wanted to know. Noise from the bar side of Straka's Tavern spilled out the open door into the street. Busy for a Saturday morning, Buck thought.

"We won!" Buck yelled and waved the newspaper in the air.

Angelo did a little cha-cha dance in the street and said, "C'mon, I'll buy you a beer and we'll see about collecting our money."

Angelo followed Buck through the door that led into the restaurant side of Straka's. Angelo kept smacking Buck on the back, to celebrate their good fortune. They rarely sat on the bar side. Too noisy and too many drunks.

Buck found a booth near the back while Angelo made a call from the pay phone by the door. The black and white tile remained polished to a shine because it wasn't yet 8:00 a.m. In a few hours, it would be scuffed and dirty, and stay that way until it was scrubbed and polished after the tavern closed to customers at 2:00 a.m. It was the only time, day or night, that Straka's closed, and they only closed because they had to.

Half-empty Heinz Ketchup bottles were switched out, salt and pepper shakers refilled, and the almost empty kegs of beer replaced with fresh ones. Both sides of the tavern, restaurant and bar, were cleaned and mopped, and prep work started in the kitchen. Trucks from the Strip District delivered meat and produce. The milk truck stopped very early in the morning, and bread arrived at four a.m. Straka's ran twenty-four-seven like the mill.

Angelo returned to the table.

"I called the cobbler, and he said my Uncle Vince can meet me here around midnight tonight. He has collections to make. After he confirms our ticket has Friday's number, he'll get the money to me."

All the tables around them were occupied and no one paid attention to them. The seating in the restaurant side, red leather upholstered booths and chairs, withstood the change of shifts for two generations of mill workers.

"Don't say that too loud," Buck said to Angelo.

"Nobody would dare," Angelo said a little louder than Buck liked. "They know who I'm related to. Besides, see that guy in the second booth from the door? The one in a suit? Old man Straka pays for protection. How do you think he cashes so many paychecks? He keeps over $100,000 here on payday. Our ten-k win is small potatoes compared to that."

"If you say so, Angelo. Last time I hit for anything substantial, I brought my neighbor's eighteen-year-old son and a couple of his friends with baseball bats with me to collect my winnings at the joint where I picked it up at in McKeesport. What is it about these numbers guys only wanting to pay out at night?"

"I told you not to be playing numbers with those McKeesport guys. They don't keep the protection in place like Homestead. Sloppy. You were lucky it was only a grand you picked up. Any more than that and they wouldn't have cared how many youths or baseball bats you had with you. Besides, nighttime is better for everyone because there's less people around and because of cops. Uncle Vince said they don't really worry about law enforcement, but they don't want to flaunt it in the cops' faces either. Less people, less problems."

"If you say so, Angelo. Let's get a shot and a beer and celebrate."

"What are you boys celebrating?" asked the waitress. Lizzie was one of the regular morning waitresses at Straka's. At thirty-five, she still smiled and moved with life and energy about her.

"Big production day, right, Buck?" Angelo looked at him and raised his right eyebrow.

"Yeah, record day," Buck said.

Angelo scanned the waitress from head to toe and back again. "How're you doing, Lizzie? Looking good."

"My shift just started, and I get you at one of my tables. How do you think I'm doing?"

"You never complained about me being at your table before. I tip generous. Lighten up, doll."

Lizzie sighed and pushed a loose curl off her face. Buck thought she had beautiful eyes and a nice figure, but would never flirt with her like Angelo did. She smiled and pulled the order pad from her apron pocket. "What can I get you guys?"

Buck spoke up: "A shot of Jack and an Iron for each of us. Any specials?"

"We have the breakfast special: a steak, three slices of bacon, a half-link of kielbasa and three eggs for $4.99. You want a menu?"

Angelo ordered: "I'll just have the burger with cheese and French fries on the side."

"I'll have the special," said Buck. "Give me the steak well done and the three eggs over easy. With toast. Buttered. Thank you. Oh, and a cup of coffee, black, with the food."

After Lizzie was out of earshot, Angelo spoke. "With my winnings, I'm buying myself a fishing boat with a trailer for Pymatuning. I've been wanting a boat for a long time. Every so often, I see pontoons advertised in the Green Sheet. Pontoons need bigger trailers, and they get you out of the sun. I'd probably find one up along the lake cheap, but they're too much work. Lots to consider. I want to fish the Yough too. I like fishing off a boat. You just drop a line and float along."

"I'm buying Peg a car. She needs her own car. The kids are getting older, and she picks up and drives them everywhere. She won't have to take me to work anymore. Louise can get her learner's permit when she turns sixteen and learn on that."

The sound of dishes crashing in the kitchen stopped conversation, but only for a beat. The volume of voices rose to its former level.

"Not to change the subject, but I heard about that Mass in your backyard with that hippie Carne from St. Joe's. I can't believe you let him do it."

"Who'd you hear it from? I didn't let him do anything. You know Peg. If she wants something, there's no denying her. Peg has unhealthy expectations of priests, and some priests, you know the kind, take advantage of that."

"People talk, Buck. Maybe you ought to switch churches. That Carne at St. Joe's got a reputation for that kind of shit. He doesn't respect the Sacrament of Matrimony. I don't know why the bishop doesn't take care of him. Monsignor should keep him in line. It is his parish, after all. Word is that Monsignor is getting too old to run a parish. Come to St. Mary Magdalene. Pastor Minichino doesn't allow folk masses. We still have one Latin mass on Sundays. Keeps out the hippies. He doesn't put up with any foolishness."

"I'm already at Saint Mary Magg's during weekday mass when Carne's on the schedule at St. Joe's. There or at St. Agnes. Peg's in Christian Mothers at St. Joe's. I'll never get her to change churches. All her friends from high school go there. We were married there. The kids were baptized there, and Louise made her first communion and confirmation there. Sammy will too. In case you hadn't noticed, I'm not Italian. St. Mary Magg's is an Italian church."

"We'll let you in. If this stuff with Carne continues, contact the bishop directly. Don't mess with going to the monsignor. If you push, you can get Carne moved. Won't be the first time the bishop moved him from what I heard."

Lizzie set the order slip on the table.

"If you say so, Angelo."

Buck understood what Angelo meant, but talking to the bishop seemed an extreme action. He wouldn't have the bishop think badly of Peg. It reflected badly on Buck, too. Angelo didn't seem to think it was Peg's fault. Maybe the bishop would understand too. Men took advantage of Peg because of her looks. He prided himself as not being like other men. He loved her for who she was, even if it meant turning a blind eye every once in a while.

"Hey boys, here's your drinks. Food orders are in. It shouldn't be too long."

Lizzie took the two full frosted mugs from the tray with one hand, set them down, then set a shot down in front of each man.

"You two said you were celebrating. Bottoms up!" she said.

Russ Doherty

Chieftain

Because I don't play music by ear—not pop, not classical, and certainly not Irish—I always have sheet music on a stand in front of me, reading the guitar chords as if I'm playing jazz in Duke Ellington's band.

It's March, 1999—I'm backing up Ciaran Finn, who performs Irish music on vocals, whistle, and accordion. We're at the grand opening of a strip mall Botox clinic in Santa Barbara and, man, is it weird, lots of fat lips and tight cheeks. Ciaran's unhappy, he's never happy, but that's another story. Today's grief is my refusal to play his normal repertoire.

Balding Ciaran plays downer Irish music: songs about war, emigration, and Irish patriots rotting in prison. Whoever hired Mr. Misery to play at this injection event has salad for brains. Ciaran's a stonemason by day, a depressed musician by night, has muscles everywhere, and his songs could bum out a Leprechaun. I only agreed to help him on this gig because my friend—his regular guitarist—has a broken arm. What a mistake I made.

"I'm singing 'Fields of Athenry' right now." He glares at me, daring me to refuse.

Oh, great, a song about famine, prison, *and* emigration. The basic trifecta of Irish sorrows.

"I don't have the sheet music. If you play that song, I'm leaving." I'm not gonna stand here doing nothing while he shows me up. And if I'd known this gig celebrated the opening of a freaking Botox clinic, I'd never have taken it.

"I've lived this life; you're only guessing what it means to be Irish." Ciaran's a head taller than me, a head case, and rearranges boulders for money. We have little in common.

He starts singing. "By a lonely prison wall . . ."

So I unplug my guitar from his PA, put it in the case, pack up my cords, sheet music, the music stand, and I'm leaving just as he finishes singing. This Botox gig sucks.

"I'm never hiring you again. You're feckin' useless."

I might be a useless Irish musician, but I'm slowly getting better. I was a good pop musician until I gave it up so I could learn Irish music with my daughter. But we only play the happy tunes: jigs and reels, waltzes and polkas. Screw his negativity.

As I walk away Ciaran pokes me in the back. "I grew up in Westport, County Mayo. You'll never be good enough to play at Matt Molloy's pub, you with your eejit sheet music. Matt will throw you out if you ever show up there." Ciaran thinks he's the Chieftain of the Santa Barbara Irish.

Well, he's not the boss of my clan.

Six months later, I'm in Ireland with my family, heading to Matt Molloy's pub in Westport.

Matt, the renowned flute player of The Chieftains, The Bothy Band, and Planxty, has parlayed his money into a famed music pub. Sinead, my thirteen-year-old daughter, is the flutist in our little group. My non-musician wife, Theresa, gives us both plenty of advice. This is my shot at the big time.

Before we left home, I told Ciaran, "I'm good enough now to play at Matt Molloy's." He laughed in my face.

As we crest the hillside we see the town laid out below us, nestled between two hills, with the Carrowbeg River running through the valley. A thundershower begins. The narrowing roadway is lined with rocks. The water dances as it funnels down to the river.

Theresa asks, "Why do you feel so compelled to show Ciaran you can do this?"

"I'm not sure. But you were right, you know, everything you said. I'm not making any money playing Irish music, and I'm broke all the time. I need to accomplish something."

Theresa says, "Why do you care about the opinions of these Irish musicians? They don't care about you. They have their own way of doing things and you might not fit in."

Inside, I feel as fragmented as ever. Wondering myself why I'm so driven. "Why can't I just go on vacation like a normal person? Why is it always about changing my life?"

In the gloom, the downpour slams our rented Vauxhall van. Frank Sinatra, on Irish radio, sings about seventeen being a very good year. I try to remember being seventeen. I'd been in the orphanage for a year, lost my only girlfriend, and had to make new friends, most of whom were pissed-off orphans. Seventeen was the worst year of my life.

Rain continues shoving water and mud onto the tarmac. Dislodged rocks, branches, broken bottles, cans, and empty cigarette packs rage past us at ever-higher rates of speed.

"Careful, the river's down there," Theresa warns me.

I head downhill anyway. As we get to the bottom and start crossing the bridge over the river, I look for our destination. The damp smell and the rolling thunder urge me to hurry.

"Sinead, get the guidebook out, find the Old Railway Hotel, quick."

The sky explodes. Above us, a waterfall tumbles from heaven. Below us, the river rises; the streets are flooding.

"Get off the damn bridge!" Theresa's totally nervous. I hit the gas, and we move off the bridge, splashing through more water.

"There it is." Sinead's spots the hotel. "We just passed it."

We're on a one-way street heading upstream, that is, uphill, away from our hotel. Spawning salmon have a better chance than we do. Somehow we get to the top of the street and I make a right, figuring there has to be a way to get back to our hotel. It'll allow everyone to relax, relieve the tension, and laugh about our latest Irish mishap.

We head down to the river.

"Don't go back down there." Theresa shakes her head.

At the bottom of the hill I part the waters, plowing back across the bridge.

"We're here," Sinead says.

The Old Railway Hotel's front door is slightly ajar. But the bottom of the door is not visible because there is a foot-and-a-half river of water flowing directly into the lobby. We have to escape now or we'll be swimming. I punch it again, and we sluggishly push upstream. Back over the bridge we go.

"Christ, you're stubborn! Why are you so insistent about playing music here?"

"I need to test myself. There's no way Ciaran is right. I can play guitar here in Ireland."

Up the hill again, same hill from two minutes ago, much more water though. Most cars have pulled over to wait out the storm. I spot a red zone and shoot into it. I turn to my right, look through the rapidly fogging windows, and spot the Holy Grail—Matt Molloy's pub—just up the street. Hallelujah.

"We need to find another hotel; there's no way we're staying at that flooded-out Railway Hotel." I splash my way out of the van, the rainstorm continuing as I wade up the street. Then I shake like a wet puppy in the pub's doorway.

"Hi there. Um, it's really pouring outside." The bartender smiles at my inarticulate understatement, raising his left eyebrow for the amusement of the one other patron. Once again, I remember why Ireland is so green and happy. It always rains and everyone's a freaking comedian. "The Old Railway Hotel has a river flowing in the front door."

"Ah, a river, is it?"

"Yeah, I need to call and cancel our room."

"Ah, now, they might be a bit busy, so."

"Do you have a phone?"

"We do, so, behind ya now." He points to an ancient instrument in the far corner. I walk over with my Fodor's guide and spend the next five minutes trying to make the phone work.

The bartender yells over from the bar. "Dial the number first. Then put the coin in."

Eventually I get a dial tone. After ringing forever, someone finally picks up.

I say, "Hi, we have a reservation." Silence. "The name's Flaherty."

"Just a bit . . . Sure you do now, here 'tis."

"But the river's flowing into your lobby."

"Ah, sure 'tis."

"So, we won't be staying there tonight."

"No, doesn't appear likely." He's probably standing on top of the reception counter.

"Would you have any suggestions for another place to stay?"

"Ah, try the Central Hotel at the top of the Octagon."

"Thanks, then."

I hang up and turn to the bartender. "He says we should try the Central Hotel, by the Octagon. Is that around here?" The patron with his back to me snorts into his Guinness. The bartender tries to suppress a laugh.

"Up the corner, turn right, first hotel on your left. Maybe a hundred meters."

Maybe . . . The patron is hunched over, his shoulders jiggling. If I didn't know better I'd say he was crying. The bartender turns away so I won't see him laughing also. I call the Central Hotel and secure a room for the evening.

As I'm leaving, I remember why we're here. "What time does the music start?"

"Half-nine."

"Thanks, see you tonight."

While we drive the hundred meters to the hotel, Theresa continues. "Is playing here really going to change your life?"

"Maybe it's just another step on the journey. I'm not sure how learning this music is going to help me, but I do know I'm lost if I don't keep moving forward. This is how I learned the blues. I forced myself to perform with musicians who were better than me. Eventually, I learned to play as good as they did."

We get to the hotel, park, and go in.

"Hi, I'm Flaherty. I just called. The river is flowing into the Old Railway Hotel."

"Sure, and doesn't it happen every year?"

"Really? Why don't they do something about it?"

"Sure, and where would they put the river?"

This is a very strange, wet country.

After a late dinner in the hotel, we grab our gear and head back to Matt Molloy's where we encounter wall-to-wall people, each with a chimney of steam coming off their still-wet clothing. It's nine-fifteen, and I can't see or hear any musicians. I use my guitar case as a battering ram to get within earshot of the bartender. Sinead's clutching her flute case.

"S'cuse me, where's the music?"

The bartender points to a room he calls the kitchen, off the main room. It's jam-packed, like an Irish wake with free whiskey.

"It's a furnace in here," Sinead notes.

The room is basically a sauna, smelling like a locker room. I spot no musicians. The crowd is loud enough to drown out a jackhammer.

"I'll get some drinks and find out what's going on." I head back to the bar. The bartender tells me the music should start any minute.

"Is Matt Molloy playing flute tonight?"

"He's on tour with the Chieftains." Of course, just my luck.

As we wait, I tell myself I'm determined to perform here tonight anyway. This is why I came back to Ireland. I'm growing and learning, putting Ciaran in his place. Finally, I hear a fiddle tuning and stand to see what's happening. Three guys are getting ready—a fiddler, a bodhran drummer, and some kind of guitar—with about fifty people crowded around them.

I force my way through the crowd, the old wooden floor dipping a bit. "Can we join you? We're musicians. We'd like to perform with you."

Silence, blank looks.

"The bartender said it would be okay." I smile the only way I know: *We are at your mercy, kind sirs.*

The fiddler looks at the guitar player. I notice it's no guitar at all; it has a rounded back and only four strings. It looks like a Greek bouzouki, sort of a Mediterranean banjo. Hopefully, we haven't walked into *Deliverance* with leprechauns.

"Sure, sit wherever you like." McFiddle shrugs at me and waves his bow for us to sit.

I go back and tell Sinead it's *Showtime*. She nods and unpacks her flute. I get out my guitar and sheet music.

As McFiddle sees us heading his way, he motions people up out of their seats so we can sit.

I'm sweating like a sinner in a confessional and can barely control my shaking. Right now I haven't the slightest idea what I'm doing here at Matt Molloy's. We get seated.

McFiddle smirks, folds his arms across his violin, and mockingly says, "Play us a tune."

The audience quiets down as my body temperature goes up ten more degrees. This is not the best idea I've had.

The bodhran player's salt-and-pepper beard matches his instrument. The hide on his drum is the actual coat of a goat; the wool hasn't been rubbed off the skin. They must be related. I'm convinced we've regressed a century or two. Sinead stares at me wide-eyed.

"Play 'Butterfly.'" I smile at her to let her know I'm not scared witless. I'm not wondering how we stumbled onto this 16th-century instrumental duel. I'm confident.

Sinead frowns slightly, taps her foot, and starts to play.

The magic happens. She begins slowly, letting the music breathe; she's clicking tonight. Her warm, minor key tones linger, washing over the room. As her notes rebound around the walls, the crowd slowly stops talking. They all stare at Sinead in disbelief. She fulfills every dream they've ever had of Ireland. The music, the essence, the beauty, the fairy dust, all flow from her flute and echo through their ears.

Her eyes close as I stare at the floor, not daring to look at McFiddle. When I come in on the B section with my quiet minor chords, the sound whispers. Breathy and soft, it's a tune as ancient and remote as the hillsides. It's apparent that Sinead is the real thing. We head back to the main theme, and I can see McFiddle knows we've won over the crowd. They're definitely pulling for Sinead in a big way.

He starts playing along with us. When I look up, he motions the bouzouki player to play also. McFiddle dances around the notes, wandering, delaying a bit, giving the music that strange unresolved pull. I scan the tourists in the room and they all have the smile, the nod, the look: *We made it, we're in the right place tonight, aren't we lucky.*

I think we've also made the leap; somehow, we're no longer musical interlopers. We're part of the Irish magic. My shoulders relax.

Ciaran can stuff his opinions. He'll find out we know what we're doing.

When we finish, McFiddle says, "Not bad." He nods to the bouzouki guy, and they take off at a hundred miles an hour. We've never heard—much less played—the reel they're flying through and even the drummer has trouble keeping up. His wool is flapping. But they sound so incredible: the leaping triplets, the octave jumps, slipping from note to note in perfect sync.

Otherworldly nuances bring back surprising memories of our last trip to Ireland. How do these dream states bubble up out of this music? Where do these musicians come from? Tonight it's a hot, crowded bar and McFiddle is putting on a concert you'd pay fifty bucks to see. His playing shames me unmercifully, yet I have to at least put out the effort to keep up with him. I try finding a tonal center for the tune. I want to eke out a few chords. As I'm getting my bearings McFiddle yells out "G" so it's obvious to everyone that I'm clueless. I try a G chord. Okay, that works. I play a few other related chords: C, F, some E minor. I'm not doing too badly when the virtuoso tune ends with a percussive *zing* on the violin.

"Good on ya, Mick," Mr. Bouzouki addresses the other two.

"Ah, yer grand yerself, there." McFiddle flicks his bow in my general direction, and he nods at my binder on the table. "What's in your book, there?"

"The tunes we play at our pub in Santa Barbara."

He furrows his dark eyebrows. "Let's have a go, like."

I need to slow the pace to at least a cross-country jog. "'Geese in the Bog,' 'Coleraine,' and 'Leitrim Jig,' okay?" They're the first three jigs we learned. He smirks as I realize they're likely the first three jigs everybody learns, only he probably learned them at age four.

"Let's . . ."

He nods and starts playing them faster than we've ever played them. Sinead and I race to keep from being left behind. The crowd seems to be getting into it now; the volume picks back up. Feet stomp in time to the music. The heat, the sweat, the closeness, all start to blend with the sound. We're murdering the tunes, but with the press of bodies, all determined to have their night of music, no one's noticing. McFiddle plays three embellished notes for every exact one that Sinead and I deliver.

We finish. Mr. Bouzouki says, "Good on ya."

"Sing us a song, so." McFiddle nods. Then he glares directly into my eyes.

He can't possibly mean me. "I couldn't sing a song if my life depended on it." I shrug and smile; he must know I don't actually *sing* Irish songs.

He stands up and leans across the table, leering at me. The crowd quiets as the sweat permeates my clothing. The smell of this pub will never leave my clothes. Why the hell am I here anyway?

Time slows way down as he says in a very loud voice, "Your life *does* depend on it."

"I . . . I don't know any Irish songs." I need a cave to crawl into, away from all these people laughing as McFiddle and Bouzouki smile and nod at each other. They are exposing me for the Irish fraud that I am.

"Sing us a song anyway." Jesus, he's not letting up. My knee starts bouncing.

It's gonna be a long night if I can't pull out of this tailspin. My ego sinks into my shoes as my mind goes blank. Think . . . Then, "Route 66" pops into my brain. I decide that'll have to do and turn to Sinead.

"Route 66."

She nods like the pro she is. The crowd noise has elevated; my ears whoosh with the sound of everyone's chatter. The buzz, the craic—whatever they call it—is happening. Everyone waits for the ultimate failure of the New Kids in Town. Sinead looks at me as if I have three eyes.

As I start playing and singing my way through the first verse, my body rocks in time to the music, back and forth. Even Mr. Goat Drummer starts slamming his hide. Things aren't looking too bad. At least I remember the words.

"Feckin' *Route 66*?" McFiddle screams out as he falls back hard onto the bench, a look of disbelief in his eyes. Well, what did he want? He's the host from hell, intimidating me in front of the crowd. Just like Ciaran. Is this some sort of an Irish musician thing?

By the time I hit the second verse people are snapping their fingers, shuffling their feet, moving their hips, singing along with the words. Who would've thought Irish tourists would dig a little swing?

I'm smiling with the crowd. We are all in this together. When I round into the last verse, they all yell out the words with me: ". . . Route sixty-six."

Da-da-da-da-da-da-da-da-dum. I end with a downward moving bass lick, then a big fat jazzy chord, and everyone in the room claps, whistles, and whoops. Watch out. I'm starting to feel like I might get accepted into this asylum.

McFiddle, however, is looking daggers at me. I wonder, *Is he friends with Ciaran?*

Such mishmash: a Greek guitar, a thirteen-year old flute player, a goat hide drummer, and a pissed-off fiddler. Even when I manage to do as I'm asked—sing a song—I still can't win.

So I nod thanks to McFiddle, motion to Sinead we're leaving, and we exit.

I'm emotionally drained. Hopefully, tomorrow will offer another chance to make our mark in Irish music.

Sinead nailed it, and yet I, the wanna-be Irish musician, can't even sing an Irish song.

So much for my shot at Irish music and meeting Matt Molloy. Ciaran's gonna be gloating if he ever finds out about this.

Nine months later we're at the Arlington Theater in Santa Barbara, about to perform with the Chieftains. It's close by Beckett's Irish Pub, where we've been playing the last four years. Because Sinead's flute teacher is the concert promoter, the Chieftains agreed we could perform the last three songs of tonight's concert onstage with them. In eight years I've gone from basically knowing nothing about this music to being allowed to get on stage with the premier Irish music group. What a complicated journey it's been to get here, onstage, with the Chieftains and Matt Molloy.

When we arrive for the concert, Sinead squeals with excitement. Theresa is calm. We stow our instruments in the green room and find our seats in the fifth row.

I gaze around the auditorium. Standing, looking back at the theater, I try to make sense of it all: the long journey, the coming home finally to my musical roots, the importance of leaving this legacy to my daughter, letting her know how much it means to me. I tell her to look back at the 2,000 people in the audience; pretty soon they'll be listening to us.

How do I explain to her the unlikeliness of this ever happening? Me, an orphan from Chicago. Somehow I end up in Santa Barbara, marry, have a daughter, and through some fluke of an epiphany and my daughter taking flute lessons I end up playing with the gods of Irish music: The Chieftains. It is so improbable. The odds, and the gods, are stacked against any normal musician achieving this.

The phrase about history repeating itself comes into my brain, and I wonder where she will be when this hits her, when her childhood memories pop out and she realizes the amazing, strange voyage we've taken. I turn away from Sinead and Theresa as my eyes start to well up. These are the steps of our lives, the tunes we dance to, and the loves we lead. Not all travel is abroad, many of our most amazing trips—and their attendant insights—occur internally.

Thankfully the concert starts and proceeds to traverse all over the map.

Paddy Moloney, the leader, plays his whistle through a few tunes, alternating with anecdotes about performing for the pope, with Sting and Van Morrison, with Tom Jones and Mick Jagger. As he starts playing his Uilleann pipes the whole band joins in.

When it's flutist Matt Molloy's turn, the notes fly so fast yet so precise it's difficult to imagine the sound coming from a human. His fingers move faster than hummingbird wings. With a burst of speed at the end of the "Kerry Fling," Matt draws tremendous applause for his apparently limitless breathing power and melodic control.

Donny Golden and Jean Butler from *Riverdance* come on and sizzle on some fast hard-shoe step-dances. Between the musicians and the dancers it's hard to keep my eyes on everyone.

"Van Morrison couldn't make it tonight," jokes Paddy as he introduces guest singer Allison Moorer, a beautiful redhead. Allison is halfway through her first song before I realize she's the singer from the *Songcatcher* and *Horse Whisperer* soundtracks. She pours southern blues out of her heart, blistering every soul in the auditorium. It brings the audience up out of their seats.

"Eh, not bad, not bad," Paddy says with his cheeky humor. He throws in a few toots of "Popeye, The Sailor Man."

When Derek Bell starts his solo piano section, I realize it's showtime. Sinead and I head over to the green room. I notice Ciaran Finn is getting up also. Who invited him to play? His wife isn't with him, but a big-lipped woman from the Botox clinic kisses him. *Is she his reward for playing at the grand opening?* He follows us.

We get our instruments and walk out on stage when Derek finishes.

My sheet music—with the tunes we've agreed to play—is stuck in the back of my pants so the audience won't notice me bringing it onstage. Ciaran notices it right away.

"Are you gonna read your eejit sheet music through your stomach there, Paddy?"

I ignore him.

Jeff White, the Chieftain's guitar player, hired just for this tour, is seated next to me. He sees me surreptitiously pull the music out from the back of my pants, drop it on the floor, and move it forward with my foot. There's no way in hell I'm making a mistake.

"I'm following you." He smiles at me, pointing to my music on the floor.

I realize he doesn't know these songs because he's a country-western player and couldn't possibly have memorized the hundreds of tunes that the Chieftains have learned over the years. So, guitar player to guitar player, I nod, it's cool, he can follow me—the consummate professional who can't remember a damned thing at this exact moment.

The set starts; the Chieftains rip into "The Salley Gardens" like we've been doing this all tour. Things are going swimmingly; though I notice Jeff White is now turned around in his chair, copying my fingering, not reading the music on the floor.

Next, Paddy Moloney switches into what is supposed to be "Over the Moor to Maggie," only it's no tune we've ever heard before. The Chieftains are playing a different tune than what we agreed to play. Us local bozos have no clue. Sinead lowers her flute.

"Don't stop playing," I say as I move my hands away from my guitar but keep strumming. I can do air guitar with the best of them. Jeff White's eyes grow big as saucers; he's plugged in, I'm not. If he stops playing it will be noticeable. No one can hear a damn thing I'm doing. How do I solve this? *Think.* I feel everyone staring me as my world shrinks.

Jeff White starts looking around like, *somebody, help me, the inmates are running the asylum.* The tune seems never ending before I realize it's in the same key as the other two tunes. I recycle the chords from the first tune and we finally get back on track. Then we head into the final tune: "Trip To Durrow." I start breathing easier.

The dancers come back out, kicking their legs and twirling their bodies to accompany the propulsive melodies of the music. The screaming audience offers rabid encouragement by clapping along in time to the rhythmic dancing.

Jeff White watches my chords the first couple of times through the tune and soon plays "Trip to Durrow" like a pro. The exuberance and immediacy of the Irish reel pulsates throughout the hall. The audience is on their feet. Hey, I could get used to this: 2,000 people screaming for the concert happening tonight.

The incredible finale goes on forever. Then it abruptly ends, fading into a mishmash of notes resembling nothing so much as the cacophony of an orchestra tuning up. The crowd goes bonkers as everyone on stage does something different. Some bow, some start talking to their fellow musicians, some hug one another. The curtain doesn't go down, but the hall lights come up, and the concert is over. The Chieftains, the Gods of Irish Music, head offstage by walking past us. Jeff White points at me as he walks past, "You saved my ass." He smiles.

Ciaran Finn stands next to me shaking his head, staring at his whistle as if it's growing hair. "Feckin' shit, I couldn't hear a damn thing. I didn't know those blasted tunes at all. I only played a D-note the whole time."

I'm usually so down on myself, but tonight my sheet music rescued us. So Ciaran's not quite the Chieftain he thinks he is. Sinead is all smiles; she's stoked.

Matt Molloy walks toward us. He must know we've played at his pub. He must know I just saved the day on my guitar. He must know this is the high point of my Irish music epiphany. He must now understand that we, he and I, and all of us here tonight, are *The Future of The Irish Culture.* He must be coming up to congratulate me—I smile and step forward.

He smiles, walks right around me, and says: "Hey, Ciaran, how are ye?"

"Okay, Matt, how ye been?" They shake hands and walk off together.

They're friends, and I'm relegated to my usual place—somewhere between nowhere and nonexistent. Life is so impermanent. But even being friends with Matt Molloy didn't make Ciaran a better musician—or a better person. I think he's missed something. The Chieftains play mostly positive, happy music that connects with the audience. Ciaran doesn't.

So many thoughts swirl through my head about getting to this point in my life. Is it an end, a beginning, or just another part of the journey? I think about Westport and how it went sideways. But tonight's concert went well. So the music is alive. It's not something preserved under glass in a museum.

And we get to continue.

Mitch James

Sorry I Could Not Travel Both

It was a gathering meant to start in the house and end around a fire. The people worked with Jermaine, all except Saul, who Jermaine had heard read at an open mic a few weeks before.

Saul.

The name had become spoken often and with familiarity, like it'd been something Jermaine and Armani had always shared together. Apparently, Saul was a pretty good poet. Jermaine said he toured the country with other poets but was on hiatus. He said they'd get to hear his work that night, and it was a blessing. Armani felt blessing an odd word from a man who didn't believe in a god.

Though Armani had yet to meet Saul, it was as if he were a kind of roommate, his name spoken more often by Jermaine than good morning or good night or how was your day, the poet's gruff lilt of a name like an aggressive secret uttered in other rooms, Armani streaming poem after poem on YouTube to see what Saul was all about. There were nights Jermaine came to bed, and he'd been crying. "I love you," he'd say through thick folds of gin. Armani wasn't sure what Jermaine loved. Him, Saul, or the poetry.

Recently, Armani realized Jermaine spoke of Saul mostly in intimate moments, like when they held each other in bed or like the other day, Jermaine swooning over Saul's poetry while he dried between his legs after a shower.

Armani always liked fiction better, the familiarity of characters suffering or dying or fleeing something. A beginning, middle, and end. You meet people in a story, and while you don't know what they'll endure, you know they'll probably change because of it. The fact there is an ending that promises to be different from the beginning, that's what Armani liked about fiction, why he read it instead of poetry. He sought cohesion, predictability, unity. Jermaine sought fragments of something larger that never pieced together the same way for two people. Armani knew without him saying it that Jermaine wanted to see the way the poets put their pants on in the morning, wanted to study the beds where they dreamed, smell the musk and day-old pot in their soiled shirts. Jermaine, he fell for poets, all of them and not just Saul. He had always been falling for poets and never the man who cooked him stew when the trees let loose their leaves.

There they were, just the two of them, Jermaine and Armani, in the kind of stillness where you hear sounds you forget your house makes, the ticking of a clock, the way a picture rattles on a wall when one walks across a room, as Jermaine did just then, to re-straighten thinly sliced medallions of cured meat into militarized lines.

The day had been cool, but as evening bore down on them, the house warmed. Armani asked if he should turn on the air, but Jermaine said no, that the breeze felt amazing. One picked their battles with their partner. Armani would die on a hill for a cause other than air conditioning.

With little pearls of sweat huddling on his own brow, Jermaine continued through the home, arranging and rearranging, pirouetting from the kitchen counter to a storage closet. Armani told Jermaine the floor was fine when Jermaine grabbed a broom to sweep up something Armani couldn't see. Finally, people began arriving fashionably late, a small fist of sweat clutching the shirt at the small of Armani's back, the AC suddenly becoming something he might die on a hill for.

People crowded in and filled small plates with cured meats, cheese, and antipasto, their fingers pinching fluted stems with bellies of wine that swallowed light, all voices becoming one, rising and falling like soft water along a shoreline. Jermaine smiled. A lot. He spoke and offered to fill others' glasses, wine corks accumulating on the counter before he added them to a bin for art projects Armani had yet to see Jermaine produce.

The conversation was a deep thick hum, discourse lubricated in red wine, but there was no Saul, only sweat. Armani felt it crawl past his waistline and down the crack of his ass. Disgusting, he thought and imagined the others feeling the same, smiling their way through it.

He knew he shouldn't but retrieved from their bedroom an oscillating fan Jermaine owned even before Armani knew him, a fan he never recalled being pulled apart and cleaned, the bright white plastic yellowed with age, the detritus of their living stretched in long folds like Merino wool across the back of the cover. Armani worked the fan into the living room without Jermaine noticing, plugged it in, and turned it on. It oscillated. No, no, it groaned with the deliberate turn of its head. The fan, in its slow yet steady rejection of everything, spit invisible remnants of their lives across the room and people and hors d'oeuvres. It was then Jermaine rounded the corner with Saul, who sauntered through their home like a sonnet recited in a Mississippi drawl, the whole of him, his body, his graying hair slipped delicately into a ponytail, clashed with the vibrant dashiki, half-tucked into jeans, and flip flops.

Jermaine grinned and touched Saul's elbow as he led him into the living room, his mouth open, about to introduce the poet to a woman he worked with. Jermaine stuttered a moment when he saw the fan. His smile, voice, his thoughts snagged like the nail bed of an exposed toe on a crack of a sidewalk. But for only a moment. He picked up where he paused and introduced Saul. Jermaine talked, then interrupted the party and encouraged everyone to move outside, where there would be a fire and music. At this announcement, Carl, who Jermaine worked with, downed his wine and headed out of the house for his guitar, a half-eaten piece of Manchego and apple slice on a plate beside the empty glass. People took their time, those close to the fan hesitant to move. "It's probably cooler out there anyway," groused a woman Armani had met once at one of Jermaine's work functions.

Jermaine ushered the group from the living room and through the kitchen with small gestures and an agreeable smile. When the last person rounded the corner, Jermaine snapped back.

"What the fuck, babe? Why would you bring that filthy thing out of the bedroom?" He yanked the chord from the wall and pinned the fan below his arm like a misbehaving child. "It's disgusting."

"Too disgusting for them but not for us?"

"They were eating food. Not sleeping in a bed. And, actually, no. It's just disgusting. It needs cleaned."

Armani didn't know why, but he followed in Jermaine's wake as if he deserved more excoriation. He always did that when in trouble.

He'd follow the person who was angry at him, who was bad-mouthing him, not just walking toward the damage but chasing it.

"Why are you right where I need to be?" Jermaine growled, storming back through the doorway, the fan at attention in the middle of the bedroom.

"I'm sorry."

"Babe," Jermaine said, stopping to take Armani's face in his hands. He kissed his forehead and gave his cheek a playful slap. "Get it together. And just do what I say." Jermaine smiled tiredly. "That's all you have to do. What I say. Then nothing goes wrong. Now let's go outside and join the party."

Armani followed Jermaine. The woman was right, it was warmer inside, an occasional breeze cooling Armani's back where sweat soaked through his shirt. Armani could hear Carl tuning his guitar before he had even rounded the corner of the house on his way to the fire ring. Some people tilted awkwardly over folded lawn chairs whose legs they struggled to spread, while others already sat and some stood in small groups, away from the tepee of kindling and stack of split wood, laboring already to talk over the sounds of chords as Carl moved from tuning to warming up. Armani stopped beside Saul, thinking, perhaps, Jermaine would introduce them, but he only inserted himself into the discussion Saul was having with Patricia, who sat in a Dick's Sporting Goods chair, a sweating IPA in her hand.

Carl paused before beginning to play. "Free Bird," someone hollered. "Boo," heckled another. The song wasn't "Free Bird" but Tracy Chapman's "Give Me One Reason." Most stopped talking at the sound of the familiar notes, while others sang along or just nodded their heads or bobbed the foot hanging over their opposite leg. Carl played three songs, all from the nineties, then Armani said, "Saul, he's a great guitarist, blues mostly, right, Saul?" He peered at Saul to confirm, his hand falling on the man's elbow. Jermaine had asked "Right, Saul" in the way lovers do when they feel emboldened to speak for their partner but aren't certain they've done justice to their appropriation.

Saul said, "I dabble," in that way all irritatingly talented people do. The modesty. The humble brag. Armani, he dabbled. Read up on American history, though it often angered him. He took free online courses with HarvardX, a few he even paid for to earn a certificate. That's dabbling. The minute Saul retrieved the guitar and refused Carl's electric tuner to, instead, tune by ear, it was clear Saul did more than "dabble."

Armani in no way considered himself a student of the blues, but he knew enough to know the way Saul played the chords was not blues. Then, as if he read Jermaine's mind, Saul said, "Though my heart's with the blues, this is a folk song." Saul picked the same few chords over and over. "It's about a man who frames another man who is, ultimately, put to death for murder. The first man owns a liquor store and spends his life selling cheap wine to the locals and trying to find a way to justify why his life as a business owner, as a person who sells cheap wine to the public, is more important than the man he framed."

Armani peered at Jermaine, who smiled at Saul despite the depressing introduction. The rest of the people seemed to be into it too, their chatter lulled to sleep by Saul's smooth and repetitive picking. Even those grouped and standing away from the fire ring moved closer. Then Saul, still picking the same chords, began to sing in a voice Armani wouldn't have thought the man capable of, given how he spoke. The voice was high and shrill, like a shard of glass cutting sorrowfully. Saul's neck looked too big to make the sounds, his shoulders too broad. He folded over the guitar as he sang, one foot on an empty chair. It was as if he must shrink and crush his voice from inside the lungs to make it wheeze in that way. It was beautiful. It was tragic. Armani couldn't contest that.

The chords and the voice ceased, and it was like the earth took a moment to inhale. All was suddenly awkward, for in that instant, the world had been a wool shawl, suffocating and uncomfortable, and now it was lifting, the cooling evening surfacing, coming back to them in pieces. The unlit kindling, saltlick grey scoliotic spines. The voice extinguished but imprint searing. The poet unfolding from origami to man. On two feet now. The world. Pieces into a whole.

Someone clapped. Armani didn't see who because he was still staring at Saul. The first clap was followed by Jermaine's. Then everyone joined in.

"It's heavy but worth a listen," Saul confirmed, aware of how he swung the mood of the gathering.

Jermaine gushed, assured Saul of how beautiful and tragic the song was, grizzly, visceral, and others agreed. As Jermaine so obviously swooned, Saul took note of something he hadn't yet. He locked eyes with Armani, and what was unfolding became evident to both men. Saul hadn't known about Armani's relationship with Jermaine. That became apparent to Armani then, too. The two stared into each other for what to Jermaine felt like an eternity, then Saul said, "I have something I'd like to recite, but I need some help. What do you say?" he asked Armani, extending him the guitar.

"I don't know how to play."

"That's okay. I can show you where to place a few fingers, and then you'll do some slow strumming. You can pick it up." Saul turned the chair beside him with his foot so that it faced Armani. "Have a seat. I'll show you."

Armani looked at Jermaine, who stared back, uncertain if Jermaine's look was curious or supportive. All others pried with eyes.

"Do it, dude," Carl urged.

A few others chimed in with soft support, so Armani sat, his heart slamming inside him like a splitting atom in search of a way out. Saul showed him how to hold the guitar and place a few fingers on the fretboard to make a chord. He had Armani strum the chord until it sounded right, then he showed him a simple transition, where he altered a finger. The sound changed just enough to be something different, though it was clear, even to Armani's untrained ear, that the new chord was birthed from that which came before, a different sound but so full of its origins it could never be entirely new.

It took only a minute or two before Armani could play the chords cleanly. Unprompted, Saul knelt and lit the bundle of paper packed beneath the kindling and sticks. The light was sudden and spastic, the sun but a cool lesion in the sky.

"That's it," Saul confirmed, his shape turning silhouette against the fire. "Just keep doing that, no matter what I do, and it'll be golden." Then, as if entering a trance, Saul turned to the fire. He wasn't looking at it or at the people or at anything at all. He was fingering through the folds of his mind as if it were a card catalog, shuffling sheaves of memories to extract those right for the moment,

112

memories that made him feel what he must embody just then. Suddenly, the shrill, shard-glass voice of the folded man boomed from his outstretched, barrel chest. Saul appeared to grow larger somehow, the fire dancing across his torso, the great eyelid pinching shut across the darkening sky.

Maybe it was the music Armani made for the first time. Or the setting. Maybe it was the power of Saul as an artist or performer. But Armani felt it, the undertow of whatever it was that attracted Jermaine to not just Saul, but the whole idea of art and beauty and those who made it. Saul loomed against the fire, it convulsive as if trying to flee or push him away. The sky was black and a shade of bruise without a name. The people, their emotions swirled in a heavy current, but their bodies were still. Armani heard but didn't listen to Saul's poem. Instead, he rode everything that was happening like one large carpet, focused on his very small but important part of the whole, the two chords he played again and again, the pulse of every heartbeat aching in the tips of his fingers as he pressed them against the frets.

After what could've been minutes or hours, Saul went silent. People relaxed, it was clear there had been a kind of tension cranked tightly in all of them. Again, it was as if there was a collective breath.

Saul turned and touched Armani's shoulder. "Perfection."

Such a simple word. Armani ceased playing. He could cry.

"I think you're a natural. You should really consider taking up guitar."

"Maybe I will," Armani confirmed. He peered at Jermaine, but he hadn't heard. He recorded the entire thing and was now uploading it to every social media account he had. Armani could see the screen. On it was everything Armani had felt, had experienced, the contrasts of light, the enamored people, Saul's poetry. But Armani, he was not there, only everything else. Saul employed a litany of words, his voice rising and falling with inflection. New angles of people's faces emerged and vanished in the dancing firelight, the whole thing a kind of organism in incessant movement, evolving, changing in the most unpredictable ways and insatiably alive. Then there was Armani, not in the shot. Just the sounds he made. Slow. Steady. The repetition of two chords. He rubbed the tip of his thumb over his fingertips, tender to the touch.

Things could only go downhill for Armani. Saul passed the guitar back to Carl, who was shy now about taking it. He played another song where he botched a couple of chords and had to restart twice because he forgot the words. One of Jermaine's other work colleagues Googled the name of the song Carl attempted to play, but the lyrics didn't match because Carl wasn't playing the song he thought he was. When it was clear Carl didn't know the name of the song, Saul proffered it, but people were already saying goodbye. Carl gave up and offered the guitar back to Saul, but he didn't take it. Instead, he told a story about traveling out West on the lecture circuit. Then he began reciting a couple of poems he read at the research institutions there. More people left. Jermaine added wood to the fire but did so poorly, so Armani resituated the logs and coals. The fire rose. Jermaine left and came back with Whiskey and glasses as the last of his colleagues said goodnight.

In a matter of moments, all had parted. There was Armani, Jermaine, Saul, and a bottle of Woodford Reserve, its belly full of firelight. The sky above was clear and, despite the fire, the moon ebullient.

"A super moon," Saul said when he noticed Armani look up.

Saul began reciting a poem. Armani didn't know if it was his or someone else's, but it was a poem about the moon. Jermaine recorded that too. When Saul finished, he took a long pull from the bottle and talked about how nice everything was, their property, how kind it was of them to open their home. When Saul described where he lived, he didn't say home. He said apartment. He said rent. There wasn't anything poetic about it, Armani thought. Saul was clearly older than both Armani and Jermaine, and Armani could hear a kind of regret in his appreciation of what Armani and Jermaine had, even if he was noting only the material elements of their lives, their home and large yard. Saul said he'd spent his formative years following art and not making money, and even then, as a man his age, some days he wanted to commit to something like they had, a relationship, a career, a home, something. But other days he only had energy for his art.

What Armani heard was that Saul didn't have the courage to commit to two things at once and so picked the easier path. He peered at Jermaine, who studied Saul and his words as if he could see both. "Two roads diverged in a yellow wood," Armani joked, remembering the valedictorian at his high school reciting the poem at graduation, though Armani remembered it being discussed in senior English as a poem about regret. It was a poem that always stuck with him, though he wasn't into poetry. Something about the many ways it could be interpreted, how it could mean so many things at once depending on what the reader brought to it. Something about how even then, before his partner, a poet, the whiskey and fire, he could still see the same yellow wood he envisioned all those years ago in his English class. That split path, it never changed.

"And sorry I could not travel both," said Saul without smiling.

They both looked at Jermaine, but he didn't know the next line.

Rebecca Brock

a woman with a hand on her hip

It was only a home test. But ever since the thing read positive, Bea
had been cleaning the house as if company were coming: she'd
changed the sheets, cleared out the guest room, swept the back patio.
Bill wasn't home and she hadn't told him yet. She checked on the
spice cake and knew it needed about fifteen more minutes. But she
set the oven timer for ten minutes anyway, just in case.

Bill was Bea's husband. They were both teachers—married
young. After eleven years, she'd assumed her life was as it was: just
the two of them. Bea liked to regularly bake deserts: brownies,
chocolate chip cookies, cinnamon rolls. They both liked to eat
things when they were hot from the oven, the centers still gooey and
thick. They were, Bea liked to say, creatures of comfort.

Tea, she said to herself as if she were her own best friend and
knew what was needed next. She filled the silver tea kettle with
water, put it on the stove to boil. She liked these better than the
electric ones in part because she could hear its whistle scream from
wherever she was in the house.

The test could have been wrong, but she doubted it. It was
something impossible falling right down into her lap.

She reached into the bread pantry and got her mother's old
porcelain teapot out from behind the toaster. She knew every edge
of the teapot from the upward angle of the spout to the handle laid
on sassy like a woman with a hand on her hip. She thought about
how a woman might make her body a shelf on which to balance
children, baskets of laundry, bags of groceries: so many uses out of
one shift of the body's weight.

They hadn't been trying to get pregnant. But they weren't doing
anything to prevent it either, which, now that Bea thought about it,
meant that they were trying.

The dress Bea wore fell to her knees: red flowers on a white
background. A dishtowel was tucked in her belt loop. The belt that
went with the dress had been lost, years ago. The teapot's shine
caught at the light and bounced a glimmer back onto her glasses,

blinded her for a moment. She thought of her mother: the sallow face nodding on the end of the thin neck. Her mother's eyes were often invisible, blotted out by the light reflecting in her thick lensed glasses, even in her coffin: a face with two squares of light, shimmering.

Bea hadn't loved her mother. She tried to say a prayer about this. But she couldn't get her throat to clear, the words wouldn't come out. She pushed her bangs off her forehead so that they stayed sticking up at an odd angle. She realized she was crying and thought, *well, it's about time*.

Her mother had been buried a year.

The tears seemed to pulse down her face, soaking through to the skin on her chest, sliding down between her breasts—like sweat, she thought. The tea kettle shrieked and she shrieked with it—the teapot slipping from her wet hands and smashing into scattered fragments. Without thinking she went to the stove, flicked the dial to off and moved the screaming thing to a burner that wasn't hot.

The teapot had been her mother's. Her mother had been alive.

Bea sat down, hard, on the floor. Her own glasses smeared and her nose running even after she used the dishtowel to wipe at it roughly. All that was left of her mother now was a twenty-two-pound cat named Lord. Bill was always tripping over the cat and muttering at it but Bea liked that he was heavy like a big pumpkin, she liked his weight on her lap. Lord was a slow, noble creature and Bea thought him a sort of miracle. She had never heard her mother's voice gentle or coax and yet the cat was sweet, even attentive—which she thought was unusual for a cat.

She tried to gather the pieces to her, feeling along the cold white linoleum for the shards of porcelain: that prick of an edge, a different sort of coolness. She had perhaps cut her knee, it was sore, and her hand was warm and sore in an unfamiliar way. She took her glasses off and wiped her face with the back of her bloodied hand. A fat black and white cat appeared in the doorway of the kitchen. The creature picked his way through the scattered sharp-edged pieces and wound himself into the weeping woman's lap. Bea took of her glasses and wiped her face back and forth against his body. The cat endured this, and the whimpering slid to a ragged sigh.

Breathe, dummy, Bea said to herself.

As a child, Bea was always breaking things. She moved too quickly, her mother said, didn't pay enough attention, her hips bumped shelves and table corners, her hands just seemed to let go of things. Her mother said if she tried to be clumsy maybe she would default into grace.

Bill liked to say that almost everything was replaceable. He believed in using things rather than keeping them locked behind glass. He used to say it loud enough for his mother-in-law to hear him. He liked watching her bristle—but he also enjoyed coming up behind the small woman, engulfing her in a bear hug and planting a kiss on her cheek. "William Lloyd," Bea's mother always said calmly. "You put me down, I'm going home this instant."

"You never do sweeten," he'd said to her, once, as she marched herself stoically out of the house, her purse in the crook of her arm, her head high.

The teapot had been off limits when Bea was a child. A teapot for guests, for special occasions, it was kept, and locked, in the kitchen hutch. Almost everything in her mother's house had been under a slipcover or behind glass. Bea remembered how the backs of her thighs would stick to the plastic covering the couch. She would wait on the front porch for her friends, and, later, for Bill to pick her up. Her father, before he moved to Florida, was there sometimes in his dark corner of the porch. But even if Bea smelled the cloves from his pipe, she didn't say hello or goodbye. She told herself she didn't want to give away his hiding place. But really, she didn't know what to say to him.

Lord was a lump of weight in her lap, the warmth of him against her stomach a comfort. She reached her hand out to pick up a rounded piece—the lid—nearly intact.

Bea wasn't sure that what Bill said about things being replaceable was true. The teapot could have been an heirloom, something to pass down. She shouldn't have been using it every day of the week for her afternoon tea. She should have been more careful.

She heard Bill's car in the driveway and she tried to wipe her face with the dishtowel again, put herself to rights. But Bill always bounded into the house, came straight to find her. "Bea? Honeybear?" he called as he came down the hallway toward the kitchen. He liked to use pet names for Bea—he said them to her as a joke when they were first married. But her blush filled him up and all these long years later he called her everything loving that he could make up or that he had heard somewhere. Every once in a while, a new name would come out of him as pretty and red as the flowers on Bea's white dress. But, upon seeing the blood, the tears, the cat and Bea in their shambles of a tableaux—he bellowed: "What in the hell?" and "Damn that Lord!"

He jerked Bea to her feet, harder than he meant too, and she came up like a large stuffed doll. Her glasses skittered under the stove. The cat lunged away and came down hard, yowling when a piece of teapot slid into his paw and stayed. "Bill!" Bea cried like an exhale as she reached for the cat, her fingers latching on fur. "Honey he's hurt," Bea put her hand on Bill's arm. Bill looked down at his blood-spattered wife, and the squirmy, mouthy cat.

"Oh, for hell's sake, give me the damn Lord," he said, but he was gentle and the cat settled against him. Bill looked at the paw, the porcelain shard sticking out like a splinter. "Hold your breath, cat," he said. The shard came out slowly, Bill applying pressure until it emerged enough that he could pull it out. Finally, Lord protested, struggled out of Bill's arms, and walked with an arched back to the remains of the teapot where he sat to tend his paw.

"He's a tough guy, this cat," Bill said, and, "What's the matter with you?" when Bea started to cry again. He tried to get a good look at her face, moving his head lower to line up with her eyes.

"I have all the pieces," Bea said. "All the parts together on the floor. I thought we could glue it."

Bill whistled one soft low note to show how he understood what she wanted. But he shook his head at the mess on the kitchen floor. "The thing I can fix up is you," he said and hoisted the solid Bea up onto the edge of the sink. He took a wet rag and began to sponge Bea's face, dabbed a cloth softly at her wounded knee—pressed a cold paper towel into her hand. He kissed each bloody part.

Bea looked down at her husband's dark head and felt the sun coming in through the window above the sink; the fade of daylight

120

faltering over her husband's back. Sometimes she wondered how she ever came to be. She couldn't remember a scene or conversation between her parents. No words—kind or harsh—just a loud silence. The first time Bea slept over at a friend's house she saw grown-ups argue. Another time, she saw them slow dance, the woman stepping out of her shoes and leaning her body into her husband's.

Maybe before Bea was even born her mother had learned that to let even a little bit of life in—a little disorder, a little mess—brought it all down on top of you. Things get broken.

Bea slid off the counter. She bumped down clumsily, the back of her thighs catching the edge, and fell against Bill. Bill caught Bea and she caught him at the same time.

Just before the spice cake's timer went off, it was quiet. Perhaps a bird sang outside the window or maybe they noticed the click of the oven's heat.

"Baby?" Bea said into the mountain that was Bill's chest, the smell of warm skin coming through his shirt. "Baby, I have some news."

Elizabeth Rosen

The Clarity of Metaphor

When I click on the e-mail from my wife, it opens to a black-and-white photo and nothing else. The photo is stark, a picture of a spindly limbed tree with no leaves on it. It is standing alone on a prairie or savannah somewhere in the world, looking, for all its severe beauty, devastating in its loneliness.

It doesn't need words. I've had years of practice interpreting, and I can guess why Ashley has chosen it. My wife thinks she's that tree. She thinks I am, too.

Even so, I sit for awhile just taking it in. My wife studied literature at college, so she's overly fond of metaphor. But not me. As comparisons, metaphors are vague and slippery, which is why I don't like them so much. They over-complicate things needlessly. I'm a guy who enjoys saying things straight out, reducing things to their essence. And the essence of my life right now is that my marriage is in trouble.

My wife and I haven't had a conversation about what's gone wrong in almost ten months. I look at the tree in that photograph and I see my wife telling me *This is what our relationship feels like*. But I also look at the tree and I think it's singularly unhelpful as an explanation. Is it the barrenness of the image she wants me to see, the bare, twisted branches, empty of life? Or is she comparing herself to the tree, alone and vulnerable? If our marriage was in a better place, if she'd sent this image to me before the trouble started, I'd be paying attention to the longevity of the tree instead, its optimistic reach skyward, its survival in the midst of an otherwise desolate plain.

I drag-and-drop the photo into the unnamed file where I keep the photos my wife has sent over the years. Around me, the noise of the cubicles never stops: binders being pulled down and opened, lacquered fingernails clicking on keyboards, the steady whir of the printer across the aisle. I like the predictability of it. It comforts me that I can stop what I'm doing and let my mind wander, as I'm doing now, and it has absolutely no effect on the hive of business around me.

I swivel in my chair so I face the opening in my cubicle. From here, I can see through to one of the manager's offices and out his windows. We're on the third floor, so this window affords a view of the corporate offices park where we're located. Sometimes, like now, there are pigeons strutting back and forth on the ledge, cocking their heads at their black-eyed reflections in the glass, trying to figure out if the bird there is friend or foe. The whole office keeps an eye on the pigeon parade in case there is unexpected drama, but there's usually not. It's just one long march along the window ledge.

I swivel back to my computer. It has misunderstood the intent behind my clicking on the file and is now pulling images from it, flashing them randomly at me in a slide show. I watch a wilting garden change to a man with a briefcase dashing across a concourse, which changes to an open padlock, keys hanging from it, which changes to a cracked egg, shell stained dirty blue with bruises. I reach out and stop the slide show on this image.

This is the image where everything started to change, the first time Ashley sent me a picture because she couldn't bear to say the words aloud. There had been more eggs since then, but this had been the first and its intent clearest. I'd sent her hopeful photos in response: cupped hands bearing a flower; a figure walking toward the blinding light at the far end of a tunnel; a close-up of a couple's hands, fingers firmly intertwined. But it didn't matter. There were fewer words after that, more images instead. I tried to keep up, to understand the layers of meaning, tried desperately to find the right image to send back that would tell her I saw her pain, that I didn't blame her, that our years together counted for something, too. But instead I just got more and more pictures of isolated figures on beaches, lonely farmhouses surrounded by foreboding mountains, single trees on empty plains.

I reach out and close the file, my own dim reflection suddenly visible on the monitor now that a dark screen with icons is all that remains.

When you're young, you hear the adults around you saying how fast time goes, but none of it sinks in until it's you, emptying out your file cabinet of the year's bills, putting new, empty folders in their places. You hold this stack of files that marks your life out in monthly statements, another step closer to owning the car, or the house, another twelve months of yard projects contracted for, of pet health records. Time marked out as IRS-friendly nuggets of financial information. You weigh the stack in your arms and think *How can I already be doing this again?*

Then you bring it all to the closet and file that year with all the years that came before and forget about it as quickly as you can because to think about it too much would be to raise troublesome existential questions that are anathema to a guy like me. In the end, a closet filled with files is the only tangible sign of all that time together.

Ashley hasn't mentioned the negative pregnancy test I found in the bathroom trash yesterday, and I refuse to bring it up. This is where we are now. The assumption that each of us is more likely to say something hurtful than loving. It's not like the beginning when you say what you mean, and if you don't, it feels like a wonderful, exciting puzzle you have to figure out, like learning a new language. Then you learn it, and you also learn it can be used for good or evil. You'd think I'd remember the moment when Ashley first said something to me and I saw it could mean something else, something cruel. You'd think that something that cuts at you like the jagged edge of a tin can would leave a mark in your memory, but maybe we've just been living this way for so long now that it all blurs together, just waiting to see if this cutting comment or the next will lead to killing infection.

Across the office, my co-workers are laughing at something; it's a pigeon pecking at its reflection. From where I sit, I can just see the half-graded construction site of the corporate offices park out beyond the bird. I'm a little surprised to realize how long the construction has been at a standstill. I've been paying attention to the pigeons and I stopped seeing the rest. Work there was halted a couple of years ago, and I guess there have been money problems since. A single excavator, its arm raised and crooked in abject prayer, still sits on the dirt, waiting to start up again.

Turning back to my computer, I open a file in the bottom corner of my screen and take from it the single image that I have had waiting there. Maybe Ashley's tree is meant to stand for our long history, or maybe it's meant to describe loneliness, but I'm tired of not knowing. I know that life is not black or white, but it is also not a stream of generalities nodding in one direction or another.

My photograph is of a Jack Russell terrier leaping over a wooden fence on the Kansas prairie. The photo captures the dog soaring joyfully over the crossbeam with just an inch to spare, its limbs stretched long and mouth wide open.

I copy-and-paste the photo into a response to Ashley and hit send, then I go to join my colleagues at the window to watch the birds.

Robert Kostanczuk

The Righteous Lemonade Crusade

The idea was to be a vision, a curiosity, to be sure. Being an inconsequential oddball wasn't the goal. It was all about becoming a difference-maker, envied by those who wished they had come up with the concept. It also was about inducing soft waves of warmth. It was about eliciting the radiance of a solar symphony.

Yes, Wendell Wykowski would prompt onlookers to think one clear thought: "There goes a self-assured person who just wants to spread a little sunshine." Older and Bolder became the giant-sized credo. There was work to be done that was fun, yet meaningful. Hungry for change in his life, Wendell Wykowski had figuratively rolled up his sleeves and was getting to work. The task would be accomplished with a crisp, lightweight suit that radiated the promise of bright summer days.

The jacket's showy vertical stripes were forest green and banana yellow. The yellow stripes, which were slightly broader, stood out. Wendell's sharply creased pants were a solid color flashing the same sunny hue. Topping off the jaunty look was a Gay '90s straw hat with a wide white band.

The inaugural stroll around the neighborhood in his finery took place on a glorious June day that reminded him of his youth. There was sensory awakening of the highest order: The smell of sweet warm grass, the cardinal's melodic chirp, the glint of sun off an iced-tea pitcher . . . it all hearkened back to nostalgic days of long ago. Whistling frolicsome tunes down the sidewalks buoyed him; "Daisy Bell (Bicycle Built for Two)" would be called into service on a regular basis.

One block from Wendell's house, a young woman washing her sporty car in the driveway offered the first feedback. "Nice suit," she beamed, giving Wendell a playful thumbs up as he passed by.

"Thank you my dear," Wendell smiled back. "That's one fine Mustang you're washing." The words came out in a slight British accent. Wendell laughed to himself: He was a blue-collar Hoosier trying to be pithy in an oh-so British way. Mr. Wykowski was more steel-mill Midwest than cosmopolitan London. His face screamed that. It was weathered, slightly puffy around the eyes, and accented by a bulbous nose reminiscent of actor Karl Malden.

Wendell felt enlivened by the success of Malden—a regular Joe from the steel town of Gary, Indiana. Malden won an Academy Award. A giant nose didn't stop Malden from becoming a star: Wendell Wykowski often leaned on that fact when life knocked him down because of his looks.

* * *

Before heading out on that first morning of the first walk, Wendell had given himself the once-over. A full-length mirror on a closet door was enlisted. The jacket was fine, but what to wear under it? "Here, try this. This will work," said his wife, Millie. She thought his outfit—and transformation—was silly, but had gone to The Gap and bought a dark green T-shirt to go with the suit. Millie couldn't bear to add more garish yellow to the mix. After donning his wife's purchase, Wendell completed the ensemble with lemon-colored socks and pearly white shoes boasting silver buckles.

"Those are very senior citizen," Millie drolly said as she gently squeezed her husband's shoulder on his way out the front door.

"Hey, I'm 66—I can't totally escape the ol' geezer duds," Wendell replied, giving a wave without looking back. The plan was to get out of the house on a regular basis to amble down the streets surrounding him and show off a bit. He would dish good cheer, and a good deed, if the situation arose. About 20 minutes an outing; that's what it would take, alternating between mornings and afternoons. Wendell thought he could hit the streets about every other day while the weather was good. Feel-good moments would be amassed by those he encountered. This, he believed, would keep him relevant.

Redemption was at hand. Who could not like the bright, solar stripes of his jacket? Wendell was recently retired. The boredom was depressing him. Things, he vowed, would change, starting on the first day for the new venture. "Hello Stanley," he shouted to a pal who was mowing his lawn. "Your grass is very healthy."

Stanley wiped his brow and honed in on Wendell's dapper outfit. "Hey, Wendell, are you in a barbershop quartet?" he queried.

"Nope," Wendell replied. "Just thought I'd wear something fun on this glorious morning." Accenting his style with a stately walking cane had been briefly entertained, but dropped, due to concern that it would be an over-the-top bauble.

* * *

The strolls were meant to be an almost daily occurrence, with one or two days being skipped each week—no need to overextend a good thing. On this inaugural day, a woman jogger in the street ran up alongside of him as he whisked his way down the shady sidewalk.

"I like your outfit; it's electric," she said, before picking up the pace and flicking a goodbye wave at him. Wendell welcomed the attention. She was slightly younger than him, and attractive in her pink tank top and matching running shorts.

"Take care, dear," he responded as she turned a corner, turning her head slightly to look back. When Wendell returned from his initial outing, Millie was at the kitchen sink.
"How did it go? What kind of looks did you get?" she asked, not looking up from washing a pan.

"It was positive; felt good," Wendell replied.

Millie was relieved, although careful not to show it. She had worried that her husband would be seen as crazily eccentric to the neighborhood, rather than well-meaning. But he seemed genuinely pleased with the trial run.

In fact, Wendell hadn't realized such a level of contentment for quite a while. Retirement from a construction job had come only a year earlier, but the void caused by being jobless had seemed to stretch into eternity. His only child—daughter Rose—was well into a marketing career that forged her independence from mom and dad.

Loneliness, and a sense of aimlessness, had been enveloping Wendell. He never dreamed he'd miss being a bricklayer so much. He often cursed the job. But it turned out such work actually constituted the good ol' days. Wendell just didn't know it at the time. Millie had grown increasingly concerned about him the last few months.

He was developing strange habits, such as spending too much

time making sure the front door was locked at night. He would stare at the deadbolt lock for a few seconds, walk away for a bit, then return and stare at it again. That ritual was repeated several times before Wendell could finally ease into his recliner for the rest of the evening and watch TV. He would also spend an inordinate amount of time washing his hands and washing dishes in the sink. Millie feared her husband had an obsessive-compulsive disorder. She prayed that his metamorphosis into a spry ambassador of goodwill would hopefully fill part of the void in his life.

If striding around the neighborhood in a loud outfit settled his fevered mind down just a little, it would all be worth it. She prayed the chaotic clothing and new persona would spin him into a better place. So far, it was working.

On one walk, Wendell let Mrs. Krylock know where he had just seen her missing dog. Mrs. Krylock found Bentley at the corner of Oak and Lincoln, just where Wendell said the beagle had been. "Thank you so much," she told him. "And, by the way, I love your clothes. We need something colorful to shake up our block." He tipped his hat to Mrs. Krylock and continued walking.

The good feeling didn't last for long, though. As he moved under a birch tree, Wendell remembered the time he had missed Rose's high school basketball game because he was too tired from work. He truly was exhausted, but regretted not sucking it up and getting to the game. She played well that evening, scoring 15 points. He should have gone. The memory made him wince. Missing her game wasn't the first time he had blown an opportunity to experience a quality moment with Rose.

A nagging notion that he could have been a better father often surfaced—like it was doing today, on his walk. The worst part was the possibility that he might have been selfish with his time, at his daughter's expense.

Selfish. That stung.

He lost his concentration and almost tripped on a bumpy piece of sidewalk in front of what used to be the old corner grocery store from his youth. He did his best to brush off the scuff mark from the tip of his glossy white shoe with quick strokes of his fingertips.

A little girl who had been playing jump rope by her house approached him. "Hey mister, I like your lemonade suit," she said with a broad smile. "It's bright as the sun."

"Well, thank you young lady," Wendell responded. "I like your pretty top with the purple polka dots." He asked her name.

"Beatrice," she answered.

"Such a lovely name," Wendell said, bending down to say the words at her eye level. The girl couldn't have been more than 9 years old. She made his day. Wendell loved the term "lemonade suit." Beatrice interpreted his getup in a spontaneous, childlike way. It gave credence to everything he was doing. Running his fingers down the buttons of his jacket to ensure that all were buttoned, the merry man in the lemonade suit resumed his walk, taking one last glance back at Beatrice. The lass had resumed jumping rope by herself. Beatrice had put a spring in his gait.

Mr. Wykowski carried on the crusade the next day, this time with a pink carnation in his lapel. There was more good cheer waiting to be dispensed. Wendell tipped his straw hat to a mailman, who was parked at a mailbox.

"Where'd ya get the outfit?" the postal worker shouted, making sure he was heard outside the confines of his vehicle.

"Got it in Florida, on vacation," Wendell said. He remembered the day well. He and his wife had stopped in a quaint clothing store in a beachfront town. The store sold some novelty clothes, such as Nehru jackets and super-flared women's pants. The striped jacket and solid yellow pants that Wendell eventually bought were on a mannequin in the back of the place. He liked the size of the jacket's stripes, about a half-inch wide for the deep green; an inch for the sun-colored band. Big and bold. He grabbed a sleeve to feel the cotton material. The suit had the seersucker look that he loved. His wife sensed he had a growing attachment to the vibrant monstrosity on the mannequin.

"You don't actually like that, do you?" Millie asked in disbelief.

"As a matter of fact, I kinda do," Wendell confirmed. Through a stroke of luck, the suit outfit accommodated his proportions. Wendell had emerged from a makeshift fitting room to model it for Millie.

"The shoulders are a tad baggy; but other than that, there's nothing major that's wrong," she said with only a whiff of enthusiasm. "The pants perhaps need to be shortened an inch." Cash was paid for the garb. Total: $279, and some change—a small price to pay for something that offered a new lease on life.

* * *

For the first three weeks of his mini-journeys, things went swimmingly for the strolling Mr. Wykowski. Some folks did double takes because of the dynamic duds. It was June 26th when Wendell took his excursions a step further, developing a theme song for them. He would play it in his head for that extra bounce.

Dating back to the 1960s, the tune was called "Hello Hello" by The Sopwith Camel. It ranked as perky, light pop-rock—a vaudevillian's delight. There also was English flavor, as if it could find favor as a sing-along in a pub across the Atlantic:

Hello, hello,
I like your smile.
Hello, hello,
Shall we talk awhile?

The song entered his noggin on an overcast day. He happened to look up through a maple tree and suddenly saw shards of sunlight breaking through the leafy canopy.

"Hello Hello" meandered into his mind. Life was getting better. But there were still many hours during the week that needed to be filled. Radiating merriment in the neighborhood wouldn't be enough, but it was enough for now.

Before heading out the door on one particularly humid day, he stuffed some bite-sized pieces of wrapped taffy into a suit pocket to hand out to children. Such an opportunity arose at the Cape Cod-style home of Ann Beastings, who was hosting a swimming pool party for her 8-year-old son and his friends. The fun was taking place on the front lawn in a small inflatable swimming pool.

"Here you go, kids. Come and get some treats," Wendell called to the children while reaching in his pocket for the taffy. The children ran to him, cupping their hands as Wendell filled them.

"What do you say kids? You tell the gentleman 'thank you,'" Mrs. Beastings yelled from the front door. She knew Wendell. They had sometimes talked home maintenance before he became the guy walking her streets in attention-grabbing yellow. She liked him, although the new clothes and personality transformation made her think Wendell was spiraling into eccentricity.

After Wendell left the pool party, he was several houses away from Mrs. Beastings' home when a harsh yell jolted him. "Hey weirdo, you gonna hand out candy at schoolyards next?" a teen boy hollered. It was Kyle Tinecki. It was around noon. Tinecki stood with two or three guy friends who were laughing across the street from Wendell. Flustered, Mr. Wykowski stopped walking and merely stared at the boys in dazed confusion. "Yeah, I'm talking to you; you're a weird dude in a weird suit," Tinecki shouted.

The whole confrontation was surreal for the Lemonade Man.

He was hurt. Stunned.

"What do you mean?" he yelled back at the tormentor. The words came out in a wavering voice.

"You're strange; that's what I mean," the teen shot back. "You keep walkin' around here in that ugly costume. You some kinda clown?"

Wendell didn't know what to say. He was mad, but more depressed. Taking a deep breath and nervously adjusting the buttons on his natty suit, Wendell started moving away. There was an effort to be unhurried, so some dignity could be salvaged. However, Wendell felt rotten. Everything had come crashing down.

The walk home seemed endless. He felt creepy. Wendell took one last look at the intruder from about a half-block away. Tinecki was still there in his white T-shirt, blue jeans and long, scraggly hair. He was wiry, with thick eyebrows and piercing eyes. He seemed to be just staring at Wendell.

It was well known in the neighborhood that Tinecki was a bad apple. He was suspended from high school more than once. Now, Wendell was experiencing for himself what school officials were facing.

At dinner that night, Millie easily sensed her husband was in another world. "You all right?" she asked over roast beef and mashed potatoes.

"I'm fine," Wendell lied, managing a tepid smile.

"Something go wrong on your walk today?" Millie knowingly asked.

"Nah, I guess I'm just kind of tired and crabby," he replied. Supper was quickly over.

"You do look tired; get some rest," Millie said, as she started clearing the kitchen table. Wendell went to bed early that night. Just before his head hit the pillow, a glance was directed toward the spreading-cheer jacket and complementary pants draped across an easy chair in the corner of the bedroom. The suit's stripes didn't seem as radiant. The straw hat on an adjoining ottoman seemed silly, as did the pearl-white "senior citizen" shoes on the floor, right below the hat. Was he a doddering old fool?

Wendell was forced to wrestle with the question. The following morning, an unexpected rush of energy got him out of bed earlier than planned. His dad used to say, "When you fall off the horse, get right back on it." It was now toasty July, and Wendell was forcing himself to don the happy suit.

About 10 minutes into his jaunt, he spotted some neighborhood kids knocking a tennis ball around the street with rackets. A coveted remembrance was shaken loose. The tennis ball kick-started a memory of him using the bouncy thing for something quite different.

"Hey, you want something new to play with that ball?" he said, entering the street for an up-close-and personal talk. "What do ya mean?" asked Chester Klapdon, an 11-year-old whom Wendell had greeted on previous walks. Asking for the ball, and then having it tossed his way, Wendell intended to give a demonstration.

"When I was a kid like you, my friends and I used to play a game in which you threw the ball downward at the point of the curb, and have it fly off," Wendell explained. "It was just a matter of hitting it against the curb — the rounded top part of the concrete curb."

Little Chester was roped in: "What was the game called?"

"We just called the game hitting it against the curb," came the answer.

"That's pretty dopey," the boy chuckled.

Wendell saw the humor. "Yeah, I guess it wasn't a very creative name," he said with a grin. "Let me see if I still have the knack." Wendell took off his jacket and handed it to one of Chester's friends to hold. The senior citizen knew he could toss the ball much better in just the T-shirt he wore underneath. Winding up his right arm, Wendell bent down to chuck the tennis ball at the apex of the curb. He hit the curb's top point, dead on. The ball flew all the way across the street.

"We'd have an outfielder standing on the sidewalk, way across on the other side of the street; if the ball went over his head, it was a home run," Wendell told Chester. "There was also an infielder in the street. If the ball came off of the curb skittering along the ground, the infielder would have to catch it cleanly or else it was an error. No baseball gloves; you caught the tennis ball bare-handed."

Chester and his buddies seemed fairly impressed at the primitive, but intriguing, game from yesteryear. "I remember the curb being somewhat rounded on the top edge that faced the street. But it wasn't rounded to the extent where it didn't have a little point — a sweet spot," Wendell said, closing his eyes as he tried to picture it in his mind. "I seem to recall the curbs we played on weren't totally smooth — they might have had a little of a gravelly surface."

Wendell noticed Chester and his friends were losing interest. "Oh yeah, just one more thing," Wendell smiled with an air of sweet remembrance. "If you didn't throw the ball with enough accuracy, it would skim the very top of the curb and shoot backwards, and you'd have to go chase it."

Putting his jacket back on, Wendell was leaving with mild optimism that Chester and company would eventually be seen trying out his new game on a summer's day somewhere down the road. But mocking chatter rolled in like jagged waves from a few yards away. It was Kyle Tinecki and his cohorts. The bully from the local high school was back. "What a dumb game from the Stone Age," Tinecki said in a booming voice.

Wendell's bounce-back moment with Chester was ruined. He said goodbye to Chester and his mates, before heading home, not looking back at Tinecki.

"Don't worry Mr. Wykowski," Chester said as he ran up to Wendell. "That idiot has bullied me before. I don't let it bother me."

Wendell answered quietly: "You're a good kid." Chester was chubby, with a thick tuft of red hair matching an exuberant disposition. "By the way, how did that kid bully you?" Wendell asked, turning back toward Chester.

"He called me fat," the boy answered. "Then he threw a rubber ball at my head, and it broke my glasses."

The man in the lemonade suit offered support, although he sensed Chester was self-assured: "You're not fat; he's just mean." Wendell left after patting Chester on the head.

Rounding a corner at the end of the block, Mr. Wykowski started feeling sorry for himself. "Why am I getting picked on?" he wondered. His thoughts were interrupted by something he felt hitting his upper back. He looked behind him and saw a huge, wet piece of wadded-up chewing gum on the ground. Then, he heard laughing and glanced over to see Tinecki running away from behind some shrubbery along the side of a ranch home. Wendell could only muster a feeble retort after becoming the target of the tossed gum.

"Stop it; just stop it," he yelled with a cry in his voice. Wendell felt vulnerable. He hated it. Taking off his jacket, he noticed a wet spot on a yellow stripe where the pink gum had struck. It was a sickening feeling. There was nothing to do but go home and gather himself.

After coming through the front door, he cried. He sat down on the living-room couch and cried. The breaking point had been reached. He wondered if the gum stain would come completely out. The stain engulfed him. There must be a way to get it totally it out, he concluded. That resolution made him feel slightly better. Wendell bemoaned how something that started out great had flipped into something freakish. A kid throwing stuff at him; that was a new low—something to feel dirty about. His hands trembled. He was afraid to go out anymore, for fear of running into the bully.

Two weeks later, Kyle Tinecki found himself wondering where the stupid guy in the yellow suit had gone. Tinecki had roamed the blocks in Wendell's old territory to inflict more torment, but the old dude was not to be seen. For just a couple of seconds, the uselessness—the sadness—of his efforts flashed across his consciousness, but not long enough to derail his mission. He'd be back.

On a weekend in the beginning of August, Tinecki headed out again. His mother spent half of the morning yelling at him; chiding him for not doing his homework, for staying out too late the night before. Tinecki thought she didn't like him much. Perhaps his father would have treated him better. But Dad was gone; he had problems with alcohol and deserted the family when Tinecki was only 9. Tinecki dwelled on his absentee father for a few minutes before rummaging around his messy bedroom for a halfway-clean T-shirt.

He found one on the floor beneath a poster of a swimsuit model. Looking into a dresser mirror, the youth pulled the hair back off his forehead to reveal two or three more pimples that weren't there yesterday. "Crap," he said to himself in disgust before hitting the streets.

The day was sunny. Tinecki's disposition wasn't. It would get even worse when he made it to Lilac Avenue, where Wendell Wykowski lived. Tinecki gazed up in astonishment at a banner strung above the street, tied to lofty tree branches. Its hand-painted lettering read: LILAC AVENUE BLOCK PARTY—MR. LEMONADE SUIT DAY. Then, the noise of the party came into focus. Kids chattering. Oldies rock 'n' roll playing. Picnic tables being moved into position . . . Smoke wafted from grills. Mrs. Krylock could be seen holding Bentley, the playful pooch found by Wendell.

Tinecki couldn't believe what was unfolding in front of him: *People were liking the aging fool!* The very idea made the young man reel. The coming together of the neighborhood on behalf of a foe was a major blow. It burned inside Tinecki's brain. The block party was essentially Chester's idea. He planted the seed for the party; his mother firmed up the concept. Chester told her he felt bad for Mr. Wykowski because he was getting picked on. Chester said all Mr. Wykowski was doing was trying to make people happy. He said Mr. Wykowski should have a party to lift his mood. Chester's mother said it should be a block party.

On an unusually cool Saturday in August, a lot of the neighborhood had turned out on the blocked-off avenue. They were backing Mr. Lemonade Suit. As Tinecki stood a few yards from the happy bustle of the bash, he felt like an outsider. "Hey young man," said a voice from behind. Tinecki snapped out of his mental fog. The voice belonged to Wendell Wykowski. "Just wanted to tell you that it's depressing being a bully," Wendell said calmly. "Don't waste time hurting people."

Wendell didn't wait for a full reaction from Tinecki. Instead, he waded purposefully into the brunt of the street-party commotion. Not looking back, Wendell heard a clipped retort from his adversary: "Go on, get out of here, old man. I don't need . . . ."

As he got farther from Tinecki, he reminded himself that the gathering in front of him was in his name. It was a godsend. No excursions by the Lemonade Man had been taken in recent days. Rather, Wendell moped about the house. The stain from the wad of bubble gum came out of his suit, though. On one rainy night—while sitting in the living room recliner—Wendell got the mark out with laundry detergent on a wet washcloth. He rinsed with another wet washcloth.

More peace of mind was supplied by the block party. Wendell came to it in a crimson polo shirt and uncool plaid shorts. But Millie showed up, carrying his yellow-and-green jacket. "Here, slip this on: How could you not wear this?" she mildly scolded.

Her husband did indeed put it on, although the colors clashed with his deep red shirt, and didn't fit those Bermuda shorts. No big deal. Wendell felt that his public still wanted to see him.

Lemonade Suit Man was not dead.

* * *

The partygoers noticed Tinecki standing at the rim of the merriment. His encounter with the Lemonade Man was over. Tinecki hung out for several minutes trying to figure out what to do. He muttered "screw it" to himself. A swell of frustration washed over him. Then, emptiness. Tinecki slowly moved away from the block party. He dropped his moist chewing gum on a nearby sidewalk in hopes it would stick to someone's shoe. Tinecki turned his gaze toward the street party. He saw Wendell Wykowski laughing with neighbors, having a good time. The old man won, Tinecki thought to himself. Tinecki was furious, depressed and restless. As he left the area, Wendell was reveling in the clear peace of mind he had attained.

Things were good. It was time to toss a yellow tennis ball against the curb. Chester and his friends were ready to give it a go. "I'll go first," Wendell said as he held the ball aloft in a celebratory moment of unbridled joy. "Chester, you play infield. Get a couple of your friends to stand at the other side of the street and play outfield.

Chester interrupted the start of the game. "I'm gonna egg Tinecki's house," Chester said proudly.

"Do what?" Wendell asked.

"Throw eggs at his house. He deserves it," Chester said earnestly while tightening his shoelaces.

Wendell was ashamed that—just for a few seconds—he thought raw eggs on his tormentor's home would be a good idea. "No, you can't do that," he reconsidered. "Promise you won't do that."

Chester gave in. He liked the old guy standing in front of him. "Nah, I won't do it," he assured.

"Why do you think Tinecki is such a bully?" Wendell asked the boy. The senior citizen was hoping a child's view could be revelatory.

"I don't know . . . I think he's just miserable," Chester shrugged.

"That's a pretty good explanation," Wendell said. He actually did think it was insightful. Wendell knew that one day he would seek out Tinecki and try to make peace with him. The affable senior citizen was somehow emotionally linked now to his torturer, for better or worse.

Alienated from the festivities of the block party, Tinecki was just about to walk through his front door. Once inside, he dipped into his refrigerator, retrieving four eggs, and gingerly placing two in the right pocket of his windbreaker and two in the left. He then strode outside with a firm sense of purpose. Damage, he vowed, would be done.

* * *

On Lilac Avenue, Wendell was returning to the business at hand after his conversation with Chester. Lost in thought for several minutes, Wendell realized he still held the tennis ball in his hand.

"Go on: Try to put it over our heads for a home run," Chester urged. "I don't think you can do it," the kid teased.

"Oh yeah, watch this," came the declaration as Wendell loosened up his right arm by rotating it in exaggerated circles. He was about to put on a show. It was game time again. Zeroing in on the curb's peak, Wendell hurled the ball down at it. There was clean contact. Wendell felt exhilaration. All was right with heaven and earth. He was winning again, just like he did as a kid. The ball bounced high into the royal blue sky. It ascended until meshing with the sun's golden glow.

Contributors & Their Inspiration

Jessica Barksdale's sixteenth novel *What the Moon Did* and short story collection *Trick of the Porch Light* were published in 2023. She's published three poetry collections: *When We Almost Drowned* (2019), *Grim Honey* (2021), and *Let's End This Now* (2024). She taught at Diablo Valley College in Pleasant Hill, California and continues to teach for UCLA Extension and in the online MFA program for Southern New Hampshire University. She lives in Vancouver, Washington.

A while back, I read a story about someone who ran a rodeo, and I wasn't sure that was even possible. After a brief Google dive, I discovered that this is the case: people own and organize rodeos. What had I been thinking? That they were governmentally subsidized? So this discovery popped up in my daily writing, and then the story came back to something I often write about, a mother failing a child, which can take so many forms. Here we have the self-involved mother trying to beat back aging and Susan, the parental child, trying to rear herself. Often this parenting is unsuccessful because as a child, well, it's hard to know what to do. Even as an adult, it's hard to know how to parent. Susan, however, makes a choice for herself.

Setter Brindle Birch is a longtime animal advocate who made her fiction debut in 2022 with the short story "For the Animals," published in the Ashland Creek Press anthology *Among Animals 3*. She shares her life with a beautiful, special, amazing cat daughter.

I wrote and rewrote different versions of "Facing Superhawk" many times over more than a decade. Inspiration came from many sources: events in history, events in the news, and personal experiences in the animal rights and "welfare" movements. In 2010 an animal shelter in Canada really did decide to carry out a mass killing because of a ringworm outbreak, and it made the news. The public was appalled and some of the animals were spared, but many others lost their lives. The Superhawk character was part of a game my sister and I used to play as children. I suppose if Superhawk had been on the scene in 2010, she would have known what to do.

Rebecca Brock is the author of *The Way Land Breaks* (Sheila-Na-Gig Editions, 2023). Her work appears in *The Threepenny Review, Bellevue Literary Review, THRUSH, Whale Road Review* and elsewhere. In 2022, she won the Muriel Craft Bailey Memorial Poetry Contest at *The Comstock Review* and the Kelsay Book's Woman's Poetry Prize. She is a reader for *SWWIM*. She has been a flight attendant for most of her adult life and is still surprised by this fact. You can find more of her work at www.rebeccabrock.org.

"a woman with a hand on her hip" began with a cat my sister rescued years ago. The cat was impossibly large (part Maine Coon? We were never sure!) and full of delicious attitude. Bea came later, the contrast between her and her mother still later. As a new mom myself, I was thinking a lot about the before of things, how some transformations come on gradually, some so impossibly sudden. I'd also been in a habit of writing dark, heavy stories and wanted to play with sweetness.

Sam Crain lives in Fremont, CA. Now that she's finished her PhD in English, she's free to return to her first love, writing stories, which she does whenever she can steal her pens back from her cats. Her stories "Debts Discharged" and "Eyes Full of Promise" can both be found on Mythic Beast Studios, where the latter was a first-prize winner.

Russ Doherty attended the Writer's Digest, Santa Barbara, and Kauai Writers Conferences. He's studied with George Saunders and Joshua Mohr. He has a double BA from UCSB in Film and Music. His work is published in *Broken Plate, Ellipsis, Evening Street Review, Glint Literary Journal, Havik, Lunaris Review*, and *The Opiate*. His short story "The Towers" is published in *Potato Soup Journal's Best of 2021* anthology.

My eight-piece Irish band, Dannsair (Dancer), played for 23 years at Dargan's Irish Pub and Restaurant in Santa Barbara. We have some 10 albums recorded, 100 or so videos on YouTube, and sheet music of the first three albums available through Mel Bay Publishing. The COVID pandemic of 2020 ended the band's journey and existence. As I was thinking over that period, I remembered some of the funnier episodes and insights that I got from performing in the band, learning and growing with the other musicians, and during various family trips to Ireland. So, I turned three of those incidents into fiction in the short story "Chieftain."

Donna Wojnar Dzurilla's work appeared or is forthcoming in the *Anthology of Appalachian Writers Volume 16, Wild Wind: Poems and Stories Inspired by the Songs of Robert Earl Keen, The Gulf Tower Forecasts Rain: Pittsburgh Poems, Backbone Mountain Review, Northern Appalachia Review,* the *Voices from the Attic* anthology series, *Rune,* the *Pittsburgh Post-Gazette, Presence,* and other publications. She shares her life in Pittsburgh with her husband Steve, and family.

"Winning in 1972" was adapted into a short story from a chapter of my novel, *Work Greens.* The novel, my MFA thesis, is set during the demise of the steel industry in Pittsburgh and explores its impact on identity (individuals and the city's) and culture of the middle class. What happens to people defined by a region's industry and livelihood when it is taken away? The main characters of Buck and Angelo, as well as Straka's Tavern in Homestead, are people and places that I know and grew up around. Playing numbers in 1972, like playing the lottery today, offered an escape from the daily grind and perhaps a chance to dream.

Karen George is author of the poetry collections *Swim Your Way Back* (2014), *A Map and One Year* (2018), *Where Wind Tastes Like Pears* (2021), and *Caught in the Trembling Net* (2024). She won *Slippery Elm*'s 2022 Poetry Contest, and her award-winning short story collection, *How We Fracture,* was released by Minerva Rising Press in January 2024. Her stories appear in *Adirondack Review, Valparaiso Fiction Review, Louisville Review,* and *NonBinary Review.* Her website is *https://karenlgeorge.blogspot.com/.*

"Ripping Off the Bandage" began with an uncomfortable phone call from a friend with whom I attended Catholic schools. She invited me to accompany her to a Right-to-Life protest which would be held on the upcoming weekend. I hadn't seen her in years, but we were Facebook friends, and I assumed she knew my pro-choice stance from my posts. It would have been easier to lie by saying I was busy that day, but I was done hiding my beliefs on women's reproductive rights. I wanted to write this story ever since that conversation, but didn't start it until after Amy Coney Barrett was confirmed for the Supreme Court in October 2020. When Roe v. Wade was overturned on June 24, 2022, I knew I had to finish it.

Mitch James is a Professor of Composition and Literature at Lakeland Community College in Kirtland, OH, the Editor-at-Large at *Great Lakes Review*, and the owner of The Write Methods (LLC), where he teaches therapeutic and creative writing modalities to guide others in experiencing the transformative power of the written word. Mitch is the author of the novel *Seldom Seen: A Miner's Tale* (Sunbury Press) and has published works across the genres of short fiction, poetry, and academic scholarship. You can find his latest short fiction in *Bull,* poetry at *Shelia-Na-Gig online,* and scholarship at the *Journal of Creative Writing Studies* and *New Writing: The International Journal for the Practice and Theory of Creative Writing*. Keep up with Mitch at mitchjamesauthor.com and Twitter (X) @mrjames5527.

"Sorry I Could Not Travel Both" is a story born of an evening of poets and musicians, all friends, sitting around a fire together. I couldn't have written it if one poet, twenty years my senior, hadn't praised my and my wife's property and life together with a tone of implicit fear that he'd missed out on something. I couldn't have written it without seeing the silhouettes of people I care about in the body of a guitar aglow with fire light. I couldn't have written it without our whiskey-soaked homage to that evening's super moon or how grateful I was for my life that night when lying down to sleep.

Jennifer Schomburg Kanke's work has recently appeared in *New Ohio Review, Massachusetts Review, Shenandoah* and *Salamander*. She is the winner of the Sheila-Na-Gig Editions Editor's Choice Award for Fiction (2022). Her zine about her experiences undergoing chemotherapy for ovarian cancer, *Fine, Considering*, is available from Rinky Dink Press (2019). Her poetry collection about mid-century gender roles *The Swellest Wife Anyone Ever Had* is available from White Violet Press. She serves as a reader for *The Dodge* and as a Meter Mentor in Annie Finch's Poetry Witch Community. She can be found on YouTube as Meter&Mayhem.

About a decade ago, my neighbor at the time was complaining about his new dog who was quite the behemoth, named Moose, who had taken to breaking into their linen closet at night and eating bar after bar of soap. This story hid in the back of my head until three years ago when I started working on a series of stories about a woman and her daughter who move from Scioto County, Ohio, to Tallahassee, Florida. The first story is "A String of Beads," in SheilaNa-Gig Editions' first fiction anthology, and this one came shortly after. Some aspects of the story are true, like how he'd gotten the dog from his ex-daughter-in-law (though she had actually wanted the dog but couldn't care for it properly since she was on active duty in the military). Oscar's personality in the story is nothing like my former neighbor's, but I did have a wildflower patch that I'm sure caused some of the folks on our street a lot of consternation.

Robert Kostanczuk is a former full-time entertainment/features reporter for the Post-Tribune newspaper of northwest Indiana. He won first place for "Best Personality Profile" in a 1992 competition sponsored by the Society of Professional Journalists, Indianapolis chapter. His beastly yarn, "A Stirring in the Woodland," was published in 2019 by *Schlock!* Webzine of the United Kingdom. Robert's flash fiction "Coming Along Swimmingly" appeared in *Beyond Words* international literary magazine (Issue 13; April 2021): Beyond Words Publishing House; Berlin, Germany. Twisted affection drenched, his short story "Steve Loved Her to Pieces," was published by *The Chamber Magazine* (February 2022). Robert lives in Indiana.

My inspiration for "The Righteous Lemonade Crusade" stems back to my childhood days when I could savor summer in all its aspects. I remembered how it filled my senses with the sun's rays reflecting off shiny objects. I remembered the sound of birds and the smell of the grass and the visions that drank in the green of nature. I just combined those factors with a tale of someone who wanted his life to stay relevant in his retirement years. I put the protagonist in the middle of summer.

Rachel Lippolis lives in Cincinnati, Ohio, with her husband and two sons. She currently stays home with them, writing after the children are in bed. Her short fiction has appeared at *Streetlight Magazine* and *The Hong Kong Review*. She was recently awarded an Individual Excellence Award from the Ohio Arts Council.

I've always felt drawn to the non-spiritual aspects of death. My late aunt married a mortician and lived over a funeral parlor. Until I was fourteen, I could look out my mom's bedroom window and see one of the largest cemeteries in the United States. It seems inevitable that I would write a story, "The Year Alice Turned Ten," about a young girl and her mother, a "mortuary cosmetologist," as they deal with the complicated emotions that arise when the girl's father returns.

Robert Pope has published many stories in journals and anthologies and three collections of short fiction, the most recent *Not a Jot or a Tittle* (2022).

My wife and I spent a lovely, arduous week in a cabin beside the Clarion River in Pennsylvania, and in the midst of this green beauty, a new fellow arrived two cabins down and began combing the grassy area in front of his cabin with a metal detector. When it beeped, he kneeled beside it and dug up some treasure as exciting as a tarnished fork. When he moved on to the space beside his cabin, Lisa couldn't imagine why he would spend his time in the forest running this machine over the dirt. To make matters worse, each time we came back from a hike, the fellow in the cabin between us spent much of his time sitting on his back porch engrossed in his phone, which must have had its own internet source as we had none. I told Lisa I would write a story about the metal detector man and spent a few hours off and on making notes to write the story when I got back home. Right off the bat, all the rest got dragged in, including the code a friend of mine and I used when I was a boy and parallels between metal detector man and the now journalist narrator. All of this began because he irritated Lisa, who made me wonder who he was and what he was looking for.

Elizabeth Rosen is a native New Orleanian, and a transplant to small-town Pennsylvania. She misses fried oyster po-boys and telling tall tales on the front porch, but has become deeply appreciative of snow and colorful scarves. Color-wise, she's an autumn. Music-wise, she's the MTV-generation. Her stories have appeared or are forthcoming in journals such as *North American Review, JMWW, Flash Frog, Atticus Review, New Flash Fiction Review, Pithead Chapel*, and others. Learn more at www.thewritelifeliz.com.

"The Clarity of Metaphor" started with a voice I liked, just a regular guy musing at his office. I'd been thinking a lot about memes and GIFs and all the short-hand images that we send each other daily. We depend on such images to accurately express our emotions and thoughts to the people we send them to, but very few images, even emojis, are so flat that they can only have one meaning. Understanding depends on context, usually knowing the sender. So I started with a regular guy who inherently understands this because of his complicated experience with his wife sending images back and forth. Similarly, it seemed right to end the story with an image that the reader would have to interpret, just as the characters in the story have been struggling to.

 Christine Sneed's most recent books are *Direct Sunlight: Stories* and *Please Be Advised: A Novel in Memos*, and she edited the short fiction anthology *Love in the Time of Time's Up* (2022). Recent stories have appeared in *Chicago Quarterly Review, Catamaran Literary Reader, North American Review,* and *New England Review*. She's also had stories included in *The Best American Short Stories* and *The O. Henry Prize Stories* anthologies. She teaches for Northwestern University and Stanford University Continuing Studies and lives in Pasadena, CA.

I can't remember the specific impetus or inspiration behind "The Last Word," but for the last eight or nine years, I've been intermittently trying to write a novel set in a bookshop. (It probably goes without saying that I've had a few false starts.) I started this short story in early 2018, but after the first couple of pages set it aside until I went back to it in the fall of 2023. Book bans were on my mind, as was the importance of books and independent bookstores, their value to our culture and communities of course incalculable.

About the Editor

John Bullock is English and has an MFA in fiction writing from the University of Virginia. His stories have appeared in the *Antioch Review, Fifth Wednesday*, the *Laurel Review, Prague Review, Clackamas Literary Review*, the anthology *Open Windows III*, and other journals. He teaches high school English in rural Ohio. *Mark Small: This is Your Life* is his first novel (Sheila-Na-Gig Editions, 2020).

Sheila-Na-Gig Editions